PURRFECT THIEF
THE MYSTERIES OF MAX 43

NIC SAINT

PUSS IN BOOKS

PURRFECT THIEF

The Mysteries of Max 43

Copyright © 2021 by Nic Saint

All rights reserved. No part of this book may be reproduced in any form by any electronic or mechanical means including photocopying, recording, or information storage and retrieval without permission in writing from the author.

This is a work of fiction. Names, characters, places, brands, media, and incidents are either the product of the author's imagination or are used fictitiously. The author acknowledges the trademarked status and trademark owners of various products referenced in this work of fiction, which have been used without permission. The publication/use of these trademarks is not authorized, associated with, or sponsored by the trademark owners.

Edited by Chereese Graves

www.nicsaint.com

Give feedback on the book at: info@nicsaint.com

facebook.com/nicsaintauthor
@nicsaintauthor

First Edition

Printed in the U.S.A

PURRFECT THIEF

At Daggers Drawn...

I think you'll agree with me that there isn't nearly enough romance in the world. And so when a young couple walked into Odelia's office, clearly in trouble, I was fully expecting a Romeo and Juliet scenario. But instead of telling us that they wanted to get married but couldn't, Casey van de Graaf and Zalman Mulhearn were there to tell us they were being forced to get married but didn't want to!

Odelia promised to talk to Casey's family to avoid this dreadful fate, but before she could, a mysterious cat burglar named John Robie stole Rudyard van de Graaf's most treasured possession, a daring theft which would soon lead to... murder. And now it wasn't just Casey who was in trouble, but the rest of her family, too. In fact it isn't too much to say that what followed was one of the most baffling cases I've ever encountered.

PROLOGUE

Rudyard van de Graaf, patriarch of the well-known van de Graaf family, had a habit, developed over the years, where he liked to savor all the things in life he enjoyed the most. In no particular order these were: a good cigar, an excellent malt whiskey, and of course his rare collection of exquisite art, acquired over a lifetime of diligent collecting. And since he was about to celebrate his eighty-sixth birthday next week, he'd managed to cram a whole lot of collecting into such a long life. He would have included women in the list of things he enjoyed, but ever since his wife Mimi had passed away, he'd decided to forego this particular pleasure, and do without female company.

And so he sat, smoking a fine cigar, sampling a vintage whiskey, and admiring the pride of his collection: the rare and invaluable Drossart Dagger. A gift from a good friend—long since deceased—it held pride of place in what he called his treasure chest, a small room adjacent to his study, where he kept the crème de la crème of his collection. An art historian, were he allowed access to Rudyard's inner sanctum, would probably be stunned when he saw the things that were gathered there in this one room. From valuable paintings, to rare pieces of China, to an entire glass cabinet filled with jewelry that had been worn by kings and queens—in fact very few mortals had ever enjoyed the pleasure of laying eyes on the rare pieces on display—all reserved for the eyes of one man only.

Rudyard hummed a contented tune as he rose from his armchair with a groan and admired his Drossart Dagger up close. The hilt of the dagger had been inset with rubies and diamonds and other precious stones, and the blade itself was as sharp now as it had been when first forged in the fires of ancient Babylon, or at least that's what the legend held. Whether it was true or not, Rudyard didn't give a damn. All he cared about was that it was as mythical as the dodo egg, and most importantly, that it was his and his alone.

Mashing out his cigar in the ashtray, and taking his tumbler into the living area of his apartment and placing it on the tray, to be carried away in the morning by a member of his household staff, he carefully closed and locked the door to his treasure room, placed the key in the top drawer of a nearby cabinet, then started preparations to turn in for the night. Half an hour later, all was quiet in the apartment, and only the regular breathing of Rudyard could be heard, interspersed with an occasional whistling sound escaping his old lungs, coated in the tar of a thousand cigars.

And Rudyard had just been dreaming about participating in a game of golf and coming out on top, as usual, when suddenly he was stirred from his dream by the sound of a click.

Instantly wide awake, he glanced around, for he'd recognized that click. It was the sound a particular wall panel made when returning to its usual position.

Odd, he thought. Almost as if… And as a sudden premonition took hold of him, he was out of his bed with an anxious snarl, shoving his feet into his velvet slippers and hurrying into his study. Glancing over to the door of his treasure room, his heart leaped into his throat and promptly collided with his uvula when he saw that the door... was ajar!

"No!" he gurgled as emotions too powerful for speech fought for prevalence in his bosom. And as he thrust open the door, the first place his eyes landed on was the glass display cabinet where his Drossart Dagger usually resided. But the dagger... was gone!

CHAPTER 1

Humans have many ways to pass the time: playing tennis, working out at the gym, dancing at a club, watching television, going to the cinema, or simply putting in their eight hours at the job and coming home to do the busywork associated with running a household. Cats, on the other hand, have only one pastime, and that is napping. It's cheap, it's easy, and anyone can do it. And, best of all, it provides you with free entertainment in the form of dreams. Yes, cats do dream. Mostly of our next meal, or, as the case may be, our next nap. So as you see, the life of your feline companion is fairly straightforward.

Except of course for this particular feline, since my human's job consists of writing stories for a living for our local newspaper, and investigating those stories and even digging deep into the kinds of mysteries that seem to plague her fellow man or woman.

And it was exactly such a case that presented itself to her when her boss Dan Goory ushered a young man and a young woman into her office—and immediately I knew that nap time was over, and that an interesting new situation was about to unfold.

For the young woman was none other than Casey van de Graaf, and the young man Zalman Mulhearn. If these names mean nothing to you, then you probably haven't read the society section of the newspaper lately, for they both hail from families as prominent as it gets. Both the van de Graaf and Mulhearn family tree go back a couple of hundred years, which is also the point in time their forebears made their fortune, and have passed said fortune onto future generations who, contrary to some, have managed not only to maintain but to increase that fortune manyfold. In other words: they're outrageously rich.

Harriet, for one, pricked up her ears immediately when the young people arrived. Harriet is my white Persian friend, and had been dozing peacefully in a corner of the office. Money means everything to Harriet, and so does social standing, and here were the scions of two families who possessed both of those much-coveted traits.

Brutus, Harriet's mate, didn't stir. The butch black cat much prefers napping to having to listen to people gab about their problems, as most people who enter Odelia's office are wont to do. And then of course there was Dooley, my best friend and comrade. He, too, had noticed the sudden intrusion upon the peace and quiet by these newcomers.

He yawned and stretched and said, "Who are these two, Max?"

"If I'm not mistaken, Dooley," I said, "and I don't think I am, these are the harbingers of something new and exciting."

"Representatives of a kibble company, are they?"

"Not exactly," I said, and glanced over to Odelia, wondering if she, too, had recognized the pair.

"Hi," said the girl, holding out a polite hand and shaking Odelia's. "My name is Casey van de Graaf, and this is Zalman

Mulhearn." She glanced over to the young man, who nodded encouragingly, as if to say: you do the talking, and I'll fill in the gaps if need be.

"Yes, of course," said Odelia. "You're the daughter of Royden van de Graaf, aren't you?"

"You know my dad?" asked the girl, much surprised.

"I interviewed him once," said Odelia, gesturing for the duo to take a seat, which they promptly did. "For our series on the great families of Hampton Cove."

"Then you probably know my parents, too," said Zalman.

"Yes, as a matter of fact I do," said Odelia with a smile. "Now how can I help you?"

"Well, the thing is, Mrs. Kingsley," said Casey, glancing to Zalman, "that we find ourselves in something of a pickle."

"So they're not kibble salespeople?" asked Dooley.

"No, Dooley, they're not," I said. "In fact I don't think they're here to sell something, but to ask for something." And Casey's next words bore this out.

"You see, Zalman and I are supposed to get married,"' said Casey.

"Oh, congratulations," said Odelia.

"No, the thing is that we don't want to get married."

"You don't?"

"Well, at least not to each other." She gave a nervous laugh. "It's a little complicated, I'm afraid."

She was very beautiful, this Casey van de Graaf, with long blond hair and refined features. Zalman, too, was no slouch in the looks department. He, too, was blond, and his face looked as if hewn from the living rock. Adonis would have been jealous had he made Zalman's acquaintance. In fact they looked as if they could have been brother and sister. And for a moment I couldn't help but wonder what kind of kids these two would put on the planet if they did get married. Perfect kids, most probably.

"So you want to get married, but not to each other?" asked Odelia, who looked intrigued at this point, as was I.

"Yes, you see, our families want us to get married, but we don't."

"There's an arrangement," said Zalman, speaking up for the first time. "An arrangement between our families for us to get married."

"The arrangement was made a long time ago," Casey picked up the tale. "Before we were born, in fact. You see, we're almost the same age, Zalman and I."

"You're a week older than me," said Zalman with a smile.

"Barely a week," said Casey, returning the smile and placing a hand on Zalman's arm. If these two weren't a couple, they definitely were close friends, that much was obvious.

"So an arrangement was made?" asked Odelia. "What kind of arrangement?"

Casey took a deep breath. "The thing is that our families are amongst the most prominent… in the state, probably. Maybe even the country."

"Not probably—definitely," Zalman corrected her.

"Well, yes, and so when our respective moms were pregnant with us, our grandads, who have always been friends, decided that the two families should be united by a wedding. And so they arranged for the two newborn babies one day to get married and in this way join the families together into one family."

"And you are those babies?" asked Odelia.

"Yes. This was twenty-five years ago now, and our grandfathers have decided that the time has come for us to honor the arrangement."

"But that's crazy," said Odelia.

"I know, right?" said Casey. "But there it is."

"It's not that I don't like Casey, Mrs. Kingsley," said

Zalman, "because I do. In fact she's one of my closest friends."

"But we don't love each other," said Casey. "Not in that way at least. In fact I've been seeing someone for some time now, and we very much would like to get married."

"Same here," said Zalman. "I've been dating a girl for the past five years."

"Only we can't, you see?" said Casey.

"Because of this arrangement," said Odelia, nodding. "But what's stopping you from simply going to your grandfathers and telling them that you don't intend to honor an arrangement that has nothing to do with you? I mean, this isn't the Middle Ages. People should be free to marry whoever they want."

"Oh, I know, and I agree with you completely," said Casey. "But the problem is that my grandfather has made certain stipulations to ensure that this wedding will go through."

"What stipulations?"

Casey shuffled in her chair. "You will treat this discreetly, won't you, Mrs. Kingsley?"

"Of course."

"Well, my grandfather has made a will," said Casey, "that stipulates that when the wedding takes place, his son—my dad—inherits. But if there is no wedding, everything will go to a charity of my grandfather's choosing. And I do mean everything."

"What charity?" asked Odelia with a frown.

"Oh, I'm sure there are several."

"So... that means that if you don't get married, your family..."

"Will be poor as church mice," said Casey, nodding. She took a deep breath. "Also, my grandfather is turning eighty-six next week, and he has said that if he dies before the wedding vows have been exchanged, the same principle applies: the family holding and all the family assets will be liquidated and everything donated to charity."

Odelia sat back. "Now that's something I've never heard before."

"No, my grandfather is what you might call an eccentric," said Casey with a nervous little laugh.

"And what about your grandfather, Zalman?" asked Odelia. "Has he made the same kind of will?"

"No, as far as I know he hasn't. He would very much like for us to get married, sure, but he hasn't made it a condition of his will as far as I know."

"In other words, he's not as crazy as my grandad," said Casey.

"Do you think he's for real?" asked Odelia.

"Oh, yes," said Casey, nodding with a grim look on her face. "Believe me, Mrs. Kingsley, my grandfather is very much for real. And if you knew him, you would understand."

"He's a serious-minded person," said Zalman. "And if I'm honest, a little scary, too."

"Or a lot scary," said Casey. "I know that when I was little, I was always scared of my grandad."

"Wow," said Odelia, and that was probably the most appropriate response.

"I know, right? So…" She glanced to her friend, who had just discovered that the office also seemed to be the home of no less than four cats. "Zalman?" asked Casey.

"Yes," said the young man, dragging his eyes away from four pairs of cat eyes regarding him very closely. He cleared his throat. "So we were wondering, Mrs. Kingsley…"

"If maybe you could have a chat with my grandfather?"

"And make him see the error of his ways."

"He won't listen to me," said Casey. "And he won't listen to my mom and dad."

"So we thought that maybe he might listen to an outsider. Someone not connected to either family."

"You mean try and shame him into changing his viewpoint?" asked Odelia.

Casey grimaced. "Something like that. You see, my grandad is very sensitive to the opinion of others. So we thought that if you were to approach him, he might see reason."

"Because if that doesn't work," said Zalman, "we just might have to get married after all."

"We could get married," said Casey, "and then wait for my grandfather to pass away, and get divorced."

"That sounds a little harsh," said Odelia with a surprised laugh.

"I know, but at this point we're both desperate."

"It was actually my grandfather's suggestion," said Zalman.

"Oh, so your grandfather…"

Zalman nodded. "He's on our side. He realizes that this is just crazy."

"Has he talked to your grandfather, Casey?"

"He has, but my grandad isn't budging. In fact since Zalman's grandfather had a talk with him, he refuses to have anything more to do with him. Says the old man has lost his marbles and must have gone mad, to change his view like that."

"He called him a traitor," said Zalman dryly.

"The problem is—and I know this sounds bad—that my grandad is in great health."

"So he might live another ten or twenty years," said Odelia, nodding.

"Maybe not twenty, but ten or fifteen? Absolutely. His doctor says he's got the heart of a man half his age." She glanced to Zalman. "And even though Zalman is a great friend, I don't want to stay married to him for ten or fifteen years, and ask my boyfriend to wait that long."

"Same here," said Zalman.

"You could of course get married, and in the meantime…" Odelia began

But both young people shook their heads decidedly. "I know what you're saying," said Casey, "and that's out of the question. My boyfriend wouldn't go for it. In fact I'd probably lose him. And also, what would people think? And what if we want to have kids?"

"Yeah, that plan pretty much went out the window the moment we thought of it," Zalman concurred.

"So you see?" said Casey. "We're at the end of our rope here."

"We don't know what else to do," Zalman said.

"There's no guarantee that your grandad will listen to me," said Odelia. "In fact the more you tell me about him the more I'm inclined to think he'll simply kick me out."

"He won't do that," said Casey decidedly. She turned to Zalman. "Will he?"

Zalman shrugged. "Anything is possible with your grandad, Case."

"Look, I'm willing to give it a try," said Odelia.

"Oh, please do, Mrs. Kingsley," said Casey, intertwining her fingers into a pleading gesture.

"And if that doesn't work?" said Zalman. "We can always threaten to jump off a roof together."

CHAPTER 2

The drive over to the large mansion that housed the van de Graaf clan was a short one—the advantage of living in a small town like Hampton Cove. Much to our surprise, though, the drive of the house was filled with police cars, and cops were swarming around as if a police convention was being hosted inside.

"What's going on here?" asked Odelia, visibly surprised that something was happening that she didn't know about.

We approached the house, and as we walked in, Odelia's husband came walking out!

"Fancy meeting you here," said Chase with a big grin.

"What's going on?" asked Odelia.

"I assumed you knew. Why else are you here?"

"I'm here to talk to Rudyard van de Graaf."

"Yeah, well, take a number," said Chase, gesturing to the cops milling about.

"He's not…"

"Dead? Oh, no. John Robie might be a nuisance, but he's definitely not a killer."

"John Robie?"

"Yeah, that's what we've decided to call him." When she continued to stare at him, he added, "The cat burglar? This is his fourth burglary in two weeks, and frankly your uncle is getting fed up with his antics."

"Oh, the cat burglar!" said Odelia, understanding finally dawning.

"Yeah, the cat burglar," said Chase. "I thought you were here for the break-in?"

"No, there's something else I need to speak to him about."

Chase waited for her to clarify, but when no explanations followed, he asked, "What?"

"I'll tell you later if that's all right with you," she said, giving him a kiss on the cheek. "Where can I find him?"

"Take the main staircase and keep going until you reach the top. That's where you'll find the old guy. Or you could take the elevator, but we've been told that's for private use only, and the housekeeper said that the old man is fussy about who uses his elevator."

"The staircase it is," said Odelia, then turned to us. "Follow me, you guys. Looks like we're moving up in the world."

"Oh, no," I muttered. I don't know about you, but I just hate staircases. It's easy for humans, because they're big, and staircases are made for them, but for us cats it's hard work to navigate all those stairs.

"What's the matter, Maxie, baby?" asked Brutus with a sneer in his voice. "Too lazy to take the stairs?"

"Not too lazy," I said. "But you have to admit it is hard work."

"I'm not admitting any such thing," said Brutus, who's something of an athlete. "Here, I'll show you how it's done," he said, and started running up those stairs as if it was an Olympic discipline and he just had to win the gold. He's like that, you see. Competitive.

Harriet, too, moved up those stairs with swift movements—even a certain grace. And then it was just me and Dooley. The stragglers, as usual.

"Let's go, Dooley," I said with a weary sigh. "I just wish they'd install elevators for cats."

"Is that a thing?" asked Dooley, much interested. He's a smallish cat, and with his short legs it's even harder for him to move up a staircase.

"I'm not sure," I said, "but if it's not, someone should invent one. I'm sure there's a big market for it."

"Or we could ask one of these nice cops to pick us up and carry us up the stairs," he suggested.

He was probably right. Cops were going up and down the stairs all the time. One of them could easily have picked us up. But unfortunately none of them spoke our language, and no matter how piteously I regarded them, even producing a sad meow, they all chose to ignore me.

So finally I decided that the best way to deal with the obstacle was simply to tackle it. Also, there was no alternative.

Sixty steps. That's how many steps we needed to climb before we reached the top of the house. Sixty! The people who design these places are definitely cat haters. There can be no doubt. Only a cat hater would put us through so much misery to go anywhere.

Finally we made it, and even though I was hot and out of breath, I couldn't help but notice that the target of Odelia's negotiations was in no mood to listen to her right now.

The old man sat in a nice comfy armchair, watching the goings-on with an incandescent eye, and when Odelia approached him and introduced herself, he waved an irritable hand and said, "I've got no time for that nonsense."

"But Casey specifically asked me to—"

"I don't care!" he bellowed. "Have you found my collection yet? No? Well, as long as you don't get me my stuff back I don't care what Casey wants or doesn't want."

"What's missing?" asked Odelia, changing tack.

"None of your business," growled the old man.

"Excuse me?"

"Fine, consider yourself excused. Now please go. And leave me to mourn in peace."

"But sir—"

"Go! Isn't it bad enough that I was robbed last night? Do you want me to die from high blood pressure by having to shout at you? No? Well, then leave. Now!"

And so Odelia walked out, her mission a big bust.

"I think we better come back later," she announced.

"Sometimes a strategic retreat is the best option," I concurred, but then I remembered those stairs. "Oh, God, no," I muttered as I stared into the abyss. If you think going up is hard for a cat, imagine how much harder it is to go down!

"Here, I'll carry you," said Odelia, and picked me up. "You, too, Dooley."

I don't think I've ever loved any human more than I did Odelia right then.

CHAPTER 3

"So what's going on?" asked Odelia once we were downstairs again. She'd found Chase in the living room, where he was in conversation with what looked like a member of the household staff. Thanking the person, he took Odelia by the arm and led her into the corridor.

"The old man got robbed," he said, "and unfortunately he's being difficult about it."

"He's refusing to tell you what was stolen?"

"Bingo."

"I already had the impression he wasn't very forthcoming with information."

"The thing is, if he doesn't tell us what was stolen, how are we supposed to find it?"

"I guess he thinks you're a miracle worker, babe," said Odelia with a grin.

"So what are you doing here?"

And so in a few short words Odelia proceeded to explain to her husband what had brought us there.

Chase whistled through his teeth. "What a story."

"Isn't it?"

"Why is it that some people can whistle through their teeth and others can't, Max?" asked Dooley.

"No idea, Dooley," I said.

"It's the shape of their teeth," said Harriet.

"I very much doubt that," I said.

"No, but it's true. The shape of their teeth and also the shape of their tongue."

"Nonsense, sparky star," said Brutus. "It's all about technique. If you master the technique, it's a cinch. Here, I'll give you a demonstration." And he actually proceeded to whistle through his teeth. "See? Easy peasy."

"Can you teach me how to do that, Brutus?" asked Dooley.

"Sure thing, Dooley," said Brutus, who was in a good mood, it seemed.

"Okay, so we better get out of here," said Chase, "and start looking for John Robie."

"So we're really dealing with a cat burglar, huh?" said Odelia.

"Yeah, I don't know how he does it, but he gets into the most secure places. Take this place, for instance. All the doors and windows were locked, and they've got a state-of-the-art alarm system in place, that is triggered the moment someone opens a door or a window. And still he managed to get in. And what's more: the old man kept his valuables locked up in a room he called his treasure chest, and kept the key in a secret place."

"Was the lock to this treasure room forced?" asked Odelia.

"No, that's the weirdest thing. The burglar took the key, opened the room, and grabbed what he could while the grabbing was good. By the time the old man woke up, what he considers the best items of his collection were gone."

"But he won't tell you what those items are."

"Nope."

"When was the break-in discovered?"

"Last night. Rudyard says he heard a noise. When he went to look, the door to his treasure chest was open, and the stuff was gone."

"Looks like I picked the absolute worst time to talk to him about his granddaughter's wedding."

"Yeah, you better come back when he's in a better mood. Though from what I can tell from talking to some of the staff, this is as good as it gets."

"You mean he's always like this?"

Chase nodded. "They call him Ruddy van de Gruff, which tells you something." A smartly dressed woman was walking up to us now, and Chase said, "I'm sorry, babe, but I'm going to have to leave you to it."

Odelia took one look at the woman and asked, "Insurance?"

"Yep. Maybe they'll be able to tell me more about what items were actually taken."

He walked off for his conference with the insurance person, and Odelia went in search of someone she could talk to about her own private mission. And I liked her thinking. Now that we were here, why not try and go about this thing in a lateral way? By attacking it from the side instead of from the front?

And to that end, she soon located the old man's son and daughter-in-law, who, contrary to Rudyard, were more than happy to talk to her, once they'd ascertained her bona fides.

"You know, Max," said Harriet, "I'll bet this is one case you won't be able to crack."

"And why is that?" I asked as we moved into what looked like the salon. A nicely appointed room, with lots of antique furniture, and plenty of gateleg tables adorned with knick-knacks and family portraits.

"Because this is the kind of case that requires a subtle

approach. In other words, the feminine approach. And since I'm the only female here, this is right up my alley."

"Are you telling me I lack subtlety?"

She laughed, going so far as to throw her head back. "Oh, Max," she said. "You have a good brain head on you, but subtlety has never been your strong suit."

"No, Maxie," said Brutus, "you are more like the bulldozer of detectives. You just go and go and go until you get your guy. And don't get me wrong, most of the time that's a good thing, but not always. Sometimes you need tact and diplomacy, and that's where Harriet excels. Isn't that right, sugar lips?"

"Absolutely, twinkle toes. And in fact I think I'll take the lead from now on, shall I?"

"You'll take the lead?" I asked, much surprised.

"I think it's for the best. You can sit this one out, Max. I'll tell Odelia that from here on out, I'm her number-one cat detective. I'm sure she'll be more than pleased."

"And why is that?" I asked with a touch of suspicion.

"Isn't it obvious? She's a female, too, Max! In case you didn't know, us females share a mystical bond."

"A mystical bond, huh?"

"Of course. In fact we don't even have to communicate. I can sense what she's thinking, and she can sense what I'm thinking, and in that sense…" She frowned, having lost the thread of her argument. "Well, anyway, we understand each other."

"Well, good for you," I murmured as she trotted up to Odelia and took her position at Odelia's feet, assuming the position of top cat.

"Maybe Harriet is right," said Dooley. "Odelia is very intuitive, isn't she?"

"I'm intuitive, too, Dooley," I said. "All cats are."

"No, but maybe it's true that Odelia and Harriet share some kind of sacred bond."

"I doubt that very much," I said with a touch of acerbity.

"He's upset," said Brutus with a grin. "It's true, isn't it, Max? You're upset. Upset because suddenly you're not the top cat anymore."

"It's not about who's the top cat, Brutus," I said. "It's about getting results."

"So if Harriet manages to solve this case, you're okay with it?"

"What case? There is no case. Odelia was asked by Casey to try and negotiate a solution to her predicament. That's not a case."

"You're such a bad loser, Max," said Brutus, shaking his head and joining his mate.

Meanwhile, Dooley and I kept our distance. After all, apparently I'd been replaced by Harriet as Odelia's top cat. Well, so be it. I sincerely wished them good luck.

Oh, who am I kidding? Brutus was right. I was upset! But since there were more important things at stake here than my bruised ego, I decided to settle in for now, and listen in on Odelia's interview.

CHAPTER 4

Royden van de Graaf was a man in his middle fifties, with a noble face, patrician nose and hair graying at the temples. His wife Abisha looked very much like her daughter Casey, with long fair hair and a fine-boned face. The couple looked very much on edge, and that was only to be understood, considering their house had been burgled last night.

"So you're not here about the break-in," said Abisha when Odelia had finished explaining what she was doing there. She looked relieved, since probably she had expected to have to tell the story of the break-in all over again. "No, but it's true. If Casey doesn't marry Zalman, Royden's dad is prepared to do his worst, isn't he, darling?"

Royden nodded. "Yeah, it might sound like a joke to outsiders, but for us it's a reality we've been living with ever since Casey was born. And no matter how hard we've tried to convince my father that he's wrong, he's adamant that this is how it's going to be."

"We've actually given up arguing with him," said Abisha. "Since it only seems to make him even more determined to push this ill-conceived idea through."

"He has always had a mind of his own, and in many ways that's a good thing, but not when it comes to the future happiness of our daughter."

"We want Casey to marry the man of her dreams, not the man Rudyard has selected for her on a whim," said Abisha. She glanced in the direction of a picture portrait that depicted Royden and Abisha and their kids. I saw that Casey had a sister and a brother. Three kids, so why was she the only one who had to deal with this ridiculous stipulation?

The same thought must have occurred to Odelia, for she asked, "How about Casey's sister and brother?"

"You mean do they also have to marry into the Mulhearn family?" asked Royden. "No. No, they don't."

"So why…"

"Why Casey?" asked Abisha. "Because Zalman's mom and I were pregnant at the exact same time. For a while it even looked as if we might give birth on the same day. But as it turns out they were born one week apart."

"That's still no reason to force them to get married."

"No, of course it isn't. There is no reason in the world why they should get married. But at the time I was pregnant, and Rita Mulhearn was pregnant, Rudyard and Cyprian Mulhearn were negotiating a business deal, and things were going so well one night, after they'd both had too much whiskey, I imagine, that they decided it would be a great idea to link both families together in a more personal way. And so they came up with this stupid plan for their grandkids to get married sometime down the road."

"I always thought arranged marriages went out of style a long time ago," said Odelia.

"You'd think so, but not in the mind of Rudyard," said Abisha.

"What happens when your father dies, Mr. van de Graaf?" asked Odelia.

Royden heaved a deep sigh. "My father has given us to understand that if he dies before Casey and Zalman have tied the knot, the arrangement between himself and Cyprian Mulhearn still stands, and in that case, the family holding will be dissolved, all assets liquidated and everything transferred to the charities of his choosing."

"Ridiculous," said Abisha, shaking her head. "Absolutely ridiculous."

"Couldn't you…" Odelia began.

"Have him declared non compos?" Abisha immediately chimed in.

"Honey!" said Royden, not eager to carry the conversation that far.

"It's a legitimate question isn't it? Is a man who wants to squander his family fortune on a whim of sound mind and body? Honestly, Royden, I don't think so. You?"

"Look, my father is perfectly fine. In fact his mind is as sharp as ever. Physically he might have some ailments related to his age, but there's nothing wrong with his brain."

"So you have looked into this possibility," said Odelia.

"Of course we have!" Abisha burst out. "Don't you think we've tried everything to get out from under this nonsense? But so far it looks as if we're stuck. And so is Casey."

"The only solution we now see is that Casey and Zalman get married," said Royden "and then immediately apply for an annulment. In that case technically they'd adhere to the letter of the arrangement, but not the spirit."

"Oh, if we tried that the old man would kick up such a fuss," said Abisha.

"Yes, but he wouldn't be able to say that we didn't do as he said. And he'd get his nice big wedding."

"He doesn't want a nice big wedding! He wants our family and the Mulhearns to be linked by blood, that's what he wants. He wants his great-grandchildren to be van de Graaf-Mulhearns."

"Or Mulhearn-van de Graafs," Royden murmured, looking as unhappy about this whole business as his wife was. Or his daughter, for that matter.

"Look, I think it's very kind of you to try and help Casey, Mrs. Kingsley," said Abisha, "but frankly there isn't anything that can be done about this."

"Like my wife says, we've tried everything."

"The only thing we haven't tried is to hit my father-in-law over the head, and hope it will knock some sense into him. But since that would probably be construed as elder abuse, we've held off on that for now."

"God, Abisha," Royden said.

"Well, you come up with a solution then," said the man's wife. "Or else you'll be walking your daughter down the aisle soon, giving her away to a man she doesn't love!"

And with these words, she got up and left the room, clearly in the throes of a great emotion. In fact it wasn't too much to say that if she didn't remove herself from the scene, she would probably hit her husband over the head.

CHAPTER 5

Royden gave Odelia a look of apology. "Excuse my wife, Mrs. Kingsley. She's pretty much had it up to here with my father."

"I tried to talk to him just now but he practically kicked me out."

"Well, he's in a bit of a state, what with this burglary and all."

"My husband gave me to understand that he's refusing to tell him what it was exactly that was stolen."

"My father hates publicity, and the last thing he wants is for the details of his collection to become known to the public. He seems to think it will attract even more thieves and burglars, and he'll lose what's left of his collection, too."

"I can assure you that my husband treats these matters with the utmost discretion."

"Oh, I'm sure he does, but try telling that to my father. You have to understand that he's from a generation who've grown up with the idea instilled in them that family is the most important thing in the world, and as a rule outsiders are not to be trusted." He shrugged. "Even I'm not sure what was stolen. So far he's refused to talk to me. The only thing I know is that what he considers the pride of his collection seems to have gone."

"And what is the pride of his collection?"

"A very unique dagger called the Drossart Dagger."

"Do you have a picture? It would make my husband's job a lot easier."

"I'm sure I could find a picture," said Royden, nodding.

"Just email it to me if you will," said Odelia. "And I'll send it to Chase."

"Just don't tell my dad," said Mr. van de Graaf with a wan smile. "He'd probably drag me over the coals if he knew I was divulging confidential information to an outsider."

"What I don't understand is that if your father is so discreet, and nobody knew what was in his collection, how did the burglar manage to steal that Drossart Dagger?"

"It's as much a mystery to me as it is to you," said Royden. "And in fact it seems that this burglar must be very well-informed. The houses of three of our friends also got hit, and the same thing happened: alarm systems mysteriously turned off, and the best objects in their collections taken. It would seem that this John Robie has some inside information."

"Do you suspect a member of your staff?"

"Right now I don't know who to suspect. Though I have to say that our people have been with us for a very long time. I very much doubt that they're implicated in any way."

"Maybe someone paid them for information about the alarm system, and about your father's collection?"

"It's possible," Royden admitted, "though unlikely, I feel obligated to say. Why would they suddenly want to sell us out now, after years of faithful service?"

It was indeed a good point, and judging from Harriet's puzzled expression, one Odelia's new top cat was also struggling with.

"Well, let's hope that it won't spoil the big birthday party," said Royden.

"Oh, that's right. Your father is turning eighty-six."

"My wife is determined to throw him a great party—one she hopes will put him in a good mood." Royden smiled. "I probably shouldn't tell you this, but her secret plan is to get the old man drunk, and then have him sign a document that will make him abandon this ludicrous idea of Casey and Zalman getting married."

"Do you think she'll succeed?" asked Odelia, also smiling.

"I doubt it. Even when drunk, my dad is always in full control of his faculties. In fact I don't think I've ever seen him lose control. Which of course is a good thing," he hastened to say. "Except when you're trying to make him change his mind about something."

Just then, two cats strode into the salon. One was a white Persian, and the other a butch black cat. For a moment they stood there, staring at us, as if not believing their eyes. Then they approached.

"What are you doing here?" asked the Persian.

"Oh, we're conducting an investigation," said Harriet, well pleased to find ourselves in the presence of the cats of the manor.

"What investigation?"

"The burglary," said her buddy.

"Oh, the burglary," said the Persian, as if it was a minor incident.

"I see you also have cats," said Odelia, as she bent down and tried to stroke the Persian's head. She deftly thwarted Odelia's attempt, though, clearly not keen on being stroked when she wasn't in the mood for it. Then again, all cats are like that, I guess.

"Yes, this is Henrietta," said Royden, pointing to the

Persian, "and the black one is Bru. I'm sure they'll get along wonderfully with your cats."

Judging from the icy looks Henrietta was giving us, that was not a foregone conclusion.

"So did you notice anything unusual last night?" I asked.

"Let me rephrase that," said Harriet. "Did you notice anything unusual last night?"

Henrietta glanced from me to Harriet, then seemed to decide that Harriet was the one in charge and said, "Nothing out of the ordinary."

"How about you, Bru?" asked Brutus.

"What's it to you?" Bru growled, not looking all that friendly.

"Um, well, we're the lead cat sleuths in this case," Brutus pointed out.

"To me you look like a bunch of intruders," said Bru. "And do you know what we do with intruders around here?" And to show us what he did do to intruders, he unsheathed one very sharp-looking claw and waved it menacingly in front of Brutus's face.

Now that's the kind of thing you shouldn't do with Brutus. In response, Brutus unsheathed his own claw and waved it in Bru's face. And to show us they meant business, they both started hissing at each other, tails distended, backs arched, and it looked as if we'd soon have a catfight on our hands!

"Oh, look at that," said Royden. "They're playing."

"Um, I think we better get out of here," said Odelia, who knew better.

"Yeah, run away, fatso," said Bru, "and never come back."

"Who are you calling a fatso, chunky?" said Brutus, and hauled off and would have hit Bru on the nose, if not Odelia had grabbed him and dragged him off.

"Come on, you guys," she said. "Time to leave."

"Yeah, you better run!" Bru yelled.

And since I had the distinct impression we'd outstayed our welcome, I decided not to ask the many questions I had in mind, but to skedaddle. For Henrietta was looking at us in much the same way Bru did. In other words, not very hospitably!

Which just goes to show: cats aren't always the cuddly creatures many people make us out to be. And since I didn't want to lose part of my fur, or receive a scratch across a sensitive body part, I hurried out in Odelia's wake, and so did Dooley and Harriet, though the latter gave Henrietta a glance that could kill. Clearly the lead cat sleuth on the case wasn't happy about being forced to beat an ignoble retreat like this.

And maybe she was right to feel upset. I don't think Hercule Poirot was ever chased away like this. Then again, Hercule never had a clawed opponent to contend with.

CHAPTER 6

We were in Uncle Alec's office, where Odelia's uncle had called an urgent meeting to deal with this spate of break-ins by the man the police had dubbed John Robie, after Cary Grant's cat burglar in *To Catch a Thief*. Like John Robie, this burglar seemed to be able to get into places that were otherwise supposed to be locked up as tightly as Fort Knox, and abscond with items of great value.

"I don't get it," said the Chief, leaning back in his chair and patting the few remaining strands of hair on his large dome. "Are you seriously telling me that Rudyard van de Graaf refused to cooperate?"

"Up to a point he did cooperate," said Chase. "But he refused to tell us what was stolen."

"But why?"

Chase shrugged. "I talked to the lady who was sent down there by the insurance company, and she said the same thing: he doesn't want us to know what was stolen."

"I don't get it. He won't get paid if he doesn't cooperate."

"That seems to be a risk he's willing to take."

"But doesn't the insurance company have an inventory?"

"Apparently some of the items that were stolen weren't on the inventory."

"Maybe they were personal?"

"Maybe."

"Well, at least we know about one item that wasn't personal," said the Chief, and brought up a picture of a very nice-looking dagger on his screen. "The Drossart Dagger, named after Otto Drossart, Prussian field officer." He looked up. "Prussia? Is that in Russia?"

"Germany, Uncle Alec," said Odelia, "not Russia."

"Oh. Well, Otto was Jewish, apparently, and was very fond of his dagger, according to this article. There's some myth attached to the dagger. Supposedly it dates back to Babylonian times, but that was probably just a tall tale Otto used to tell his friends. More likely the dagger was made for Otto by a master Berlin craftsman. A real work of art, and reportedly worth a fortune. After Otto died in 1853 the dagger stayed in his family, until it disappeared sometime during the war. Hasn't been seen since. Until now, apparently."

"So this is what his son called the pride of his father's collection," said Chase, as he studied the picture.

"Very valuable piece of art," said Uncle Alec.

"According to this, the dagger was stolen from the Drossart family by the Nazis," said Chase. "And like you said, they never did get it back after the war."

"The Nazis, huh?" said Uncle Alec. "So how did it end up in the private collection of Rudyard van de Graaf?"

"When did Rudyard acquire the dagger?" asked Chase. "Did his son know?"

"I didn't ask," said Odelia. "But if you want, I can call him."

"Let's hold off on that for now," said Uncle Alec. "Frankly I don't care if he got the dagger from Adolf Hitler himself. All

I want is to catch this John Robie, and you," he said, pointing to Chase and Odelia, "are going to make that happen. Is that understood?"

"Uncle Alec looks a bit nervous, Max," said Dooley.

"That's because he's under a lot of pressure," I explained. "When the rich of Hampton Cove are having their most valuable items stolen, and even their expensive alarm systems are unable to keep this cat burglar out, they're not going to be happy, and they're going to complain to the Mayor, and the Mayor will complain to Uncle Alec, and now Chase and Odelia are going to have to make sure that this doesn't happen again."

"And that those valuables are returned without delay," Harriet added. "Oh, for your information, I've decided to change my name. From now on you can call me VI Harriet."

We all stared at her.

"Like VI Warshawski?" she clarified. "It sounds so much cooler, don't you think?"

I didn't, but I wasn't going to risk Harriet's ire by telling her.

"What does the VI stand for?" asked Brutus, who was as surprised as we were.

"Very Important, of course," said Harriet.

"I don't think VI stands for Very Important, Harriet," I said.

"Well, it does. But since Very Important Harriet is too much of a mouthful, I've decided to shorten it to VI Harriet. And I expect you to call me that from now on, is that clear?"

"Yes, Harr—VI Harriet," I said dutifully.

"And now please shut up. I can't hear what they're saying."

"So what about me?" asked Odelia.

"What about you?" asked Uncle Alec.

"What do you want me to do?"

"I thought I made myself clear: I want you and Chase to team up and find John Robie."

"But what about my promise to Casey van de Graaf?"

"What about it?"

"At least I have to try to make her grandfather change his mind."

"You can do that in your own time," said Uncle Alec with an impatient gesture of the hand. "I'd like to make it clear that John Robie is now our number one priority. As long as this guy is on the loose, no one is safe. And we can't have that. Is that understood?"

"Yes, Chief," said Chase.

"Yes, Uncle Alec," said Odelia.

"Good. Now get lost—and get me some results!"

But before we could get lost, suddenly the door burst open and Gran and Scarlett walked in. Judging from the serious expressions on their faces, Odelia's grandmother and her friend were on the warpath.

"What do you want?" asked Uncle Alec, with a distinct lack of a son's love for his sweet old mother.

"We want what's owed us," said Gran, and pounded the desk with her fist for good measure.

"You promised us more cooperation, Alec," Scarlett explained.

"Yeah, more cooperation between your police force and my neighborhood watch," Gran added.

"Our neighborhood watch," Scarlett amended.

"But instead of more cooperation, we're getting less!"

"I really don't have time for this," said the Chief, looking more and more harried. In fact he looked like one of those volcanoes, just before they're about to erupt and drop a pile of lava on the unsuspecting town at the foot of the hill. Steam was pouring from his ears and I thought I could hear a rumbling sound. Though that could have been my stomach. We'd been on the road for some time now, and I was getting a little peckish.

"We want a decent patrol vehicle," said Gran, giving the desk another thump. "And we want uniforms with a nice logo. And we want night-vision goggles, stun guns, pepper spray, listening devices, the works. So we can finally do a proper job and make sure this John Robie character doesn't make any more victims."

The steam abruptly stopped streaming from Uncle Alec's ears, and the rumbling stopped. "Catch John Robie?" he asked, now looking like a pointing dog, his nose up as if he'd just sniffed something good. A nice rabbit, perhaps, or a fat pigeon.

"If only you took us more seriously, Alec," said Scarlett, "we would have caught this guy by now."

"I never thought I'd say this," said Uncle Alec, "but you may have a point."

"Of course we have a point!" Gran cried.

"So how about it?" said Scarlett. "Can we finally get some decent equipment so we can do a proper job?"

"Let me think about it," he said, but he definitely looked like a man who was ready to buy. Or sell. Or whatever he was going to offer the neighborhood watch in exchange for a firm commitment to put a stop to John Robie's burglarious activities.

"Fine," said Gran. "But don't think too long."

"Yeah, we're going out tonight," Scarlett said, "and we can't do it without a decent car."

"And night-vision goggles."

"And stun guns and pepper spray and—"

"Yeah, yeah, yeah," said Uncle Alec. "I said I'll think about it. Now get lost, all of you."

And so we all got lost. Gran and Scarlett to come up with

a plan of campaign to catch the cat burglar, and Chase and Odelia… to do the exact same thing.

Even VI Harriet was on the case. And Brutus, of course, VI or not.

With such a pool of talent, John Robie didn't stand a chance!

CHAPTER 7

Odelia had decided to drop by Casey van de Graaf's place and give her the bad news. These things are like band-aids: better to rip them off without delay.

VI Harriet and Brutus had decided to join Gran and Scarlett, and prepare tonight's patrol and catch John Robie, so it was just me and Dooley riding in the car with Odelia.

Her old pickup made strange rattling noises, but apart from that it was rolling along nicely, and since it was just the three of us, Odelia had allowed us to ride in the front, which was a lot nicer than in the back, I can tell you.

"So are you giving up trying to convince Casey's grandad?" I asked.

"I'm not giving up," she said as she steered her pickup along the road. "Just trying to come up with a new angle."

"I liked Casey's mom's plan," said Dooley. "Give the old man a conk on the head."

"That kind of thing only works in cartoons, Dooley," said Odelia with a smile. "In real life when you smack a person on the head what happens is that they go to the hospital and you go to jail."

"Oh," said Dooley, much sobered.

"There must be a way to make that man see the light, though," I said. "Presumably he loves his granddaughter, right?"

"I wouldn't be too sure about that," said Odelia. "A man who puts business before family doesn't have a lot of love to give in my opinion."

She was right, of course. This whole arrangement started as a business deal, with two unborn babies as bargaining chips. And now, twenty-five years on, two young people were the victims of one man's ambition. It was not very nice, and in fact a little troubling.

We arrived at a brand-new apartment complex, and Odelia parked right in front. Once inside, we were quickly ushered in by Casey, who had tied an apron in front of her, and had something stuck to her hair that could only be cake batter.

"Come in, quick!" she said as she hastened in the direction of her kitchen. "I'm baking a cake!" she yelled. "Or at least that was the plan. I'm not sure if it will be edible."

We moved through to the kitchen—always a place that captures my attention, but to my disappointment I saw no evidence of any pets: no bowls and no cat flap either. Which meant no food for Dooley and me. And now I was really getting hungry!

"How did it go?" asked Casey as she checked something in the oven, then frowned. "I followed the recipe but it doesn't look anything like that YouTube video."

"Following cooking videos rarely does," said Odelia. She sniffed the air. "It sure smells good, though."

"Doesn't it? If I could, I'd bake cakes all day, just for the smell. I'd give them to the neighbors, though."

"Because they're so bad?"

"No!" laughed Casey. "Because if I keep them I'd eat them all. I just love cake."

We all retreated into the salon and Odelia and Casey took a seat. Casey sitting cross-legged and Odelia quickly removing her shoes when she realized how nice the carpets were in Casey's apartment. "So I talked to your grandfather," she said, "or at least I tried to talk to him."

"Uh-oh. That doesn't sound promising."

"I don't know if you've heard, but there was a break-in last night."

"A break-in? You mean, at my parents' place?"

"Yeah, looks like it was a cat burglar who's been targeting people for a while now. John Robie?"

But Casey shook her head. Clearly she hadn't heard of this famous cat burglar.

"Anyway, they stole some stuff from your grandfather, so he was in no mood to talk to me about the arrangement—or anything else, for that matter."

Casey had placed a hand to her mouth. "My grandpa was robbed? But that's terrible!"

"He's not too happy about it, I can tell you."

"What did they take?"

"He doesn't want to say."

"Typical."

"The only thing we know for a fact is that a valuable dagger was stolen."

"Oh, that's right. He has this old dagger. It looks expensive."

"Has he had it a long time?" asked Odelia, her natural curiosity aroused.

"As long as I can remember. I have to be honest, though, I've only seen it once. Grandpa doesn't like it when people visit his treasure room. And the only time I did see it was when he'd left the door to the room open by mistake. The fact that I was only six at the time may have saved my life." She grinned. "He did give me an earful, though."

"He did seem very upset this morning when the police asked about it."

"He was probably more upset that cops were crawling all over his treasure room than the fact that his dagger was stolen," said Casey with a laugh. "Do you know that he sits in that room at night, just staring at that dagger? Just like Thomas Crown in his private viewing room, when he's looking at that stolen painting."

"You don't think your grandpa stole that dagger, do you?"

"Oh, no, of course not."

"Look, I'm not giving up, Casey. But I think it's best to wait until he's in a better mood."

"Yeah, of course." She sighed. "It's just that... my boyfriend is getting a little anxious. He proposed to me again. The third time already."

"Congratulations."

"He keeps proposing to me, and I keep telling him the same thing: I can't say yes, because I have this family thing hanging over my head."

"Have you told him about the arrangement?"

"Oh, sure. He knows all about it."

"And what does he say?"

"He thinks it's idiotic, and it is. But idiotic or not, it's still a real threat to my family. I mean, I can't very well go ahead and marry him and then watch my family being turned out on the street, all of their money going to charity. And of course I'm sure there are many great causes that could use the money, but for us to lose everything like that..."

"How did your family make their money, if I may ask?"

"You may," said Casey with a grin. "The first van de Graaf made his fortune with oil, and then as time went on, invested his profits in a number of ventures. And bought up a ton of real estate, of course."

"As one does."

"Right now the family's portfolio consists of all kinds of different companies in different industries. Though I'm sure Grandpa would be able to give you a rundown. He's always had a head for numbers."

"Is he still active in the family business?"

"Of course. Van de Graafs never retire. They're like the pope: they keep going until they drop dead."

"And your mom and dad?"

"All active in the family business. Every family member is, actually."

"Even you?"

Casey smiled. "Why? Don't I look like a hardened businesswoman to you?"

"You don't, actually."

"I'll take that as a compliment. I work mostly with my dad at the office. He's training me to take over one day, I guess. We go into the office a couple of times a week, and we also work from home."

"And your siblings?"

"Well, Royce is also working at the main office in New York, commuting with me and Dad, but Emma is too young. She's still in college. Though when she graduates she'll have a job waiting for her."

"Must be fun, working with your mom and dad."

"It is—and it isn't. Dad might not look like much of a disciplinarian, and at home he isn't, but at the office, it's pretty clear who's the boss. Though when Grandpa drops by —he still has his own corner office, even though he only goes in once a week now—he likes to take hold of the reins. Hard for him to let go, you know, after all those years."

Odelia stuck her nose in the air and sniffed. "And now if

you don't mind, I think I'd like to sample that cake. It smells absolutely delicious."

"Oh, you're a very brave woman, Odelia Kingsley," said Casey with a grin.

Too bad cats don't eat cake, because otherwise it would have been a cake festival, since Casey had made a lot. And judging from the yummy sounds the two women made, it wasn't so bad after all.

CHAPTER 8

After Odelia had her cake—and ate it, too—she decided to return to the office and put in some work for tomorrow's edition of the Gazette. The public were so fascinated by this cat burglar that she couldn't provide them with fresh content fast enough. And of course now she had a name to call the dastardly fiend: John Robie.

And so after we'd finally had a bite to eat, we tripped out of her office to have a chat with one of our main sources of information: the always very well-informed Kingman.

Kingman's human runs the General Store, and is not only a good friend but also the unofficial mayor of Hampton Cove. He knows all and sees all—and loves to talk about it.

"I'm not sure what to think of this whole cat burglar business," said Kingman, who had taken up position in front of his store as usual.

"What do you mean?" I asked.

"Well, he's giving us cats a bad name, isn't he? In fact I wanted to ask you guys a big favor."

"Sure," I said. "What is it?"

"We all know that public opinion in this town is largely

formed by Odelia, with the articles she writes for the Gazette. So maybe you can ask her to coin a new phrase."

"A new phrase?" I asked, not seeing where Kingman was going with this.

"Dog burglar," he said. "Get rid of this whole cat burglar business once and for all. And if she uses 'dog burglar' often enough, you'll see that people will adopt the term, and hopefully we'll be able to rid ourselves of this blot on the good name of cats everywhere."

"It's an idea," I admitted. "Though I doubt whether Odelia has as much clout as you seem to think. Nowadays people are more influenced by social media than regular media."

"Yeah, I guess you're right," said Kingman. But then his round face lit up. "Oh, I know! Maybe Odelia can create a meme. Memes are all the rage, aren't they? She can create a meme of a dog burglar and start spreading it on the Gazette's social media channels. I'm sure that people will pick up on it and make it go viral in no time." He gave us a serious nod. "Viral is the secret, boys. Make something go viral and you're on velvet."

"Mh," I said, not hiding my lack of excitement for his scheme. Odelia may be a popular reporter, but her capacity to make things go viral is limited, as far as I'm aware. In fact a ten-year-old kid can probably make things go viral a lot faster than an established reporter nowadays. There's no rhyme or reason why one thing goes viral and another sinks like a stone in the billions of uploads on all of those social media outlets.

"I don't think the term 'dog burglar' will be very popular, Kingman," said Dooley, adding his voice to the discussion.

"And why not?" asked Kingman, eyeing a female feline who was sashaying across the street.

"Because dogs don't crawl across rooftops like cats do. And this burglar is crawling across rooftops and shimmying up drainpipes and doing all the kinds of things only cats can do—not dogs."

"Mh," said Kingman. "I guess I hadn't looked at it that way."

"In fact that's probably why they call them cat burglars: because they move with the same grace and acrobatic prowess as a cat."

We both stared at Dooley. "Prowess?" said Kingman with a grin. "What did you have for breakfast, Dooley? A thesaurus?"

"There was an item on the news last night about the cat burglar," he said with a touch of diffidence. "And they talked a lot about his acrobatic prowess. I looked it up and it's an actual word, prowess. And it does have a nice ring to it."

"Well, I guess you're right," said Kingman with a sigh. "Dogs don't shimmy up drainpipes or crawl across rooftops. So cat burglar it is. Though I still think John Robie is giving cats everywhere a bad name, and the sooner he's caught and locked up, the better."

"Chase and Odelia are on the case," I said, "but it's not easy to catch this man. He seems to be able to gain access to places and disable alarm systems like nobody's business. It's uncanny."

"Inside job," Kingman said with a knowing nod. "Has to be. Disabling alarm systems and knowing exactly where to find the loot? Gotta be someone who's got the inside track."

"You mean like a member of staff?" I asked.

"Sure. A butler or a secretary. Something like that."

"Could also be someone who works for the insurance," I said musingly. "They know what there is to steal, and where to find it—and they know what items are the most valuable. Though Chase said that in Rudyard's case the insurance company wasn't made fully aware of some of the items that were stolen. Rudyard didn't have them insured, apparently.

Like the Drossart Dagger. There's definitely something fishy about that."

"Well, I'm sure Odelia and Chase will figure it out," said Kingman.

"Actually Odelia is working on a different case," I said, and told Kingman about Casey van de Graaf's problem with her grandpa.

"An arranged marriage, huh? You'd think that kind of thing went out of style a long time ago."

"It's not as if he's actually forcing her to marry Zalman," I said.

"Oh, yes, he is. If she doesn't marry the guy she'll be responsible for her family's misfortune. So what about this Zalman? Is his grandfather also going to leave his entire fortune to a charity of his choice when his grandson doesn't marry the girl he selected?"

"I'm not sure. I had the impression the Mulhearn patriarch isn't as strict as Rudyard."

"So what if Zalman simply refuses to marry Casey van de Graaf? Nothing she can do about it. Force majeure, in other words. And then she can go to her grandad and tell him: look, I tried to do what you said, but the other guy doesn't want me! Tough luck, gramps!"

"I don't think it's as simple as that," I said.

"Rich people. They're weird," said Kingman.

"And now that his dagger was stolen, Mr. van de Graaf is even more unreasonable," said Dooley. "So he won't budge, even if Casey has an excuse for not wanting to get married to Zalman."

"I'm sure that things are not as bad as they seem," said Kingman. "After all, this guy probably doesn't want his entire family fortune that he worked so hard to preserve to be squandered on some silly cause."

"Those charities aren't some silly cause," I said. "I'm sure they're carefully selected and could do with a nice influx of cash."

"Who couldn't!" Kingman cried. "I would be happy with the money. In fact maybe next time you visit this lunatic you can suggest he pick me as the beneficiary of his will. If he's going to scatter riches to the four winds like some madman, it might as well be me!"

I laughed. "What would you do with the van de Graaf millions, Kingman?"

"Buy Wilbur a nice little condo on some tropical island so he can retire."

"I doubt whether Wilbur would be happy on a tropical island. He loves his store."

"That's what you think! You go and tell Wilbur right now that he can close up shop and move to the Caribbean and he'll go down on his bare knees and thank his lucky stars!"

"But Wilbur loves his shop. He loves his daily conversations with his customers. He enjoys being in the center of things. He's part of what makes this town so unique."

"Unique is right," Kingman grunted. Wilbur's hyena-like laugh reached our ears, and when we glanced up at the storeowner, we saw that he was watching a Droopy cartoon, laughing loudly at one of the gags. In fact he was laughing so hard he was actually slapping his thighs—something I'd only ever read about, but had never seen before.

The customers, as they stood in line, exchanged knowing glances. Yep, Wilbur sure was unique. In fact he was so unique he was almost like an institution—or a curio.

And just when I was going to touch upon some of Wilbur's other quirks, suddenly a police car zoomed up to the curb, a window rolled down, and Odelia yelled, "Max, Dooley—get in!" And so we did as we were told, and moments later were racing away. Chase, who was driving the car, clearly made haste, and when I glanced over, I saw that Harriet and Brutus were also in the car.

"They picked us up as we were strolling along," Brutus explained with a shrug.

"Obviously they realized they needed their top sleuth on the case," Harriet said.

"Case? What case? What's going on?" I asked.

"There's been a murder," said Odelia curtly.

"Murder! Who? Where? How?"

"Rudyard van de Graaf was stabbed to death in his study. And guess what?"

"What?!" I cried, much surprised at this denouement.

"Looks like he was stabbed with the Drossart Dagger."

CHAPTER 9

And so we found ourselves back at the van de Graaf home, only this time in much graver circumstances. This time not some precious possessions had been taken, but a life.

When we arrived, we were immediately led upstairs, to the old man's study. And indeed there he lay, surrounded by a bunch of books that he must have dragged down when he fell, since a table had been upended. The cause of death wasn't hard to figure out: the dagger was still very much in evidence, sticking out of the man's chest.

Abe Cornwall, the country coroner, sat hunched over the body, giving it a thorough once-over. When we entered he looked up. "Ah, the Kingsleys. I'm afraid this man is dead."

"I figured as much," said Chase as he approached. Odelia, meanwhile, studied the fallen stack of books and the upended gateleg table. Both she and Chase were donning plastic gloves and one of those plastic coveralls, making sure their DNA wasn't being spread all across the crime scene. For us, no such measures were taken, though I could have told them that cats do shed, and all that cat hair might hamper the investigation.

Dooley must have thought the same thing, for he said, "Shouldn't we be wearing those plastic coveralls, Max?"

"I was just thinking the exact same thing, Dooley," I said.

"I mean, we're dealing with a cat burglar here, Max, and if our cat hair gets mixed up with the cat burglar's hair, they won't know which is which."

I stared at him for a moment, but he was serious. "Cat burglars aren't actual cats, Dooley," I finally pointed out. "So if they shed hair, it will be human hair."

"Oh," he said, puzzled. "I didn't think of that."

"Which is why you should let me and Brutus do the thinking," Harriet pointed out. "In fact I think you better remove yourselves from the scene. We'll take it from here."

And so we were expertly ushered out of the room, prohibited from conducting our investigation!

"Harriet is really taking this sleuth business seriously, isn't she, Max?" said Dooley.

"Yeah, I guess she is," I said, not too well pleased with this development.

In the corridor, we almost bumped into Henrietta and Bru, the van de Graaf cats.

"Oh, look what the cat dragged in," Henrietta sneered.

"Where are the other two?" asked Bru.

"In there," I said. "Conducting an investigation into the murder of your human."

"Rudyard wasn't our human," said Henrietta with a touch of disdain. "In fact he wasn't anybody's human. Except of course the dogs he used to own over the years."

"All dead now," said Bru with marked glee.

"He used to own Chow Chows," said Henrietta. "Silly mutts."

"Did you notice anything out of the ordinary? Anything that could shed some light on Rudyard's murder?" I asked, deciding to strike while the iron was hot.

The two cats shared a quick glance, then Henrietta said, "We did see the van de Graaf ghost again last night."

"The van de Graaf ghost?" I asked, wondering if she was pulling my leg.

"Yes, he was very active again," Bru confirmed. "He's the ghost of the first van de Graaf, you see. Rolf van de Graaf. Who established the family fortune and built this house. He died a long time ago but his ghost lives on and has been haunting this place ever since."

"Do you think it was the ghost that did it?" asked Dooley, much impressed by this story.

Both Henrietta and Bru nodded seriously. "Absolutely,' said Henrietta. "You see, Rolf probably didn't like the way Rudyard was running things. And so of course he killed him."

"Oh, dear," said Dooley. "You better tell VI Harriet. She's in charge of the investigation."

A sly smile crept up Henrietta's lips, then was gone again, replaced by her customary stoic expression. "Oh, I will. I'll tell VI Harriet all about it."

"Dooley!" I said, once they were gone. "You're going to ruin Harriet's investigation."

"What do you mean? She needs to know that there's been a breakthrough in the case. The ghost did it!"

"There's no such thing as ghosts, Dooley. Can't you see they're messing with us?"

"They are?"

"Of course!"

"Oh."

Odelia and Chase now stepped out into the corridor, and moments later we followed them down the stairs—those stairs again!—and soon found ourselves in conference with Rudyard's son and daughter-in-law. Also present was Casey's younger sister, who'd found her grandfather's body. Emma looked very much shaken, which was only to be expected.

Meanwhile, Harriet and Brutus had remained upstairs, presumably pumping Henrietta and Bru for more information on the ghost of Rolf van de Graaf.

"So you found your grandfather, Emma?" asked Odelia gently.

Emma nodded. She was as fair-haired as her sister and mother, but of stockier build. She took after her dad in that respect, who was also a more beefy figure than his wife.

"I did," said Emma. "It was horrible."

"How did you happen to be here?"

"Grandpa sent me a text, telling me he needed to see me about something important. Here," she said, handing over her phone. "I thought it was about this whole business with Casey and the wedding, so I got here at four o'clock, and found him…" Her voice faltered, and a tear slid from her eye. Her mom handed her a tissue, which she gratefully accepted.

"Did you see anyone?" asked Chase. "On the stairs? Or in the elevator?"

"I took the stairs," said Emma. "I didn't see anyone."

"When did it happen?" asked Royden.

"According to the coroner it must have happened between three and four, so just before Emma arrived," said Chase. "Were you both at home?"

"No, I was at the office," said Royden. "I took the chopper as soon as I heard."

"The chopper?"

"Yes. We always commute by chopper. We have a helipad in the backyard. Though we often stay in town, too. We have a place in Manhattan, just around the corner from the office."

"Fun lifestyle," I murmured.

"I was here," said Abisha. "I actually opened the door when Emma arrived."

"Which was at four o'clock?"

"Yes, maybe a little before four." She frowned. "'You don't seriously believe we had anything to do with this, do you?"

"I'm sorry, but the sooner we eliminate you from the investigation, the sooner we can focus on the actual perpetrator," Chase explained. "It's a routine part of the investigation."

Abisha nodded, but didn't look convinced.

"So how do you think the murderer got in?" asked Odelia.

Royden shrugged. "I have no idea. He could have gotten in through the backdoor, or even through the verandah. We don't lock the doors during the day, only at night."

"There's no security people to guard the house?"

"No, we don't bother with that kind of stuff. Look, I explained all this to you this morning, when you were here about the burglary. No, we don't employ security people, but we do have cameras set up to guard the perimeter, and we have a contract with a security company who keeps an eye on things. And we have an alarm system, of course."

"We'll check the CCTV footage, if that's all right with you."

"I'm not sure what good it will do, since John Robie was careful enough not to be caught on camera last night, and I'm sure he will have been clever enough not to be caught on camera today, when he came back to murder my father."

"So you think John Robie killed your dad?" asked Odelia, wrinkling her brow with concern.

"Yes, of course it was him. Who else could it have been? My father was killed with his own dagger, a dagger that was stolen by John Robie."

"But why would he return with the dagger to kill your father?" asked Chase.

"Because he wanted to finish the job. He managed to grab some valuable stuff last night, and when he did, he was probably surprised how extensive my dad's collection actually was. So he decided to return today, to grab some more, only this time my dad must have caught him at it. There must have been a struggle, and in that struggle Robie struck down my dad with the first thing he could get his hands on: that damn dagger."

"But why would he bring the dagger?"

"How should I know? The mind of these people works differently than the mind of the non-criminal element, doesn't it? Maybe he was so enamored with the dagger that it has become a permanent part of his outfit? Maybe he uses it to pry open doors and windows? That's for you people to find out. All I know is that Robie crossed a line. Until now all he did was rob people. But now he's become a killer." Royden wagged a finger in Chase's face. "If you had caught him sooner, Dad would still be alive. So his death is on your head!"

"Royden, please," said Abisha. "This isn't helping."

"But it's true, isn't it? If he'd been caught sooner…" His voice broke, and soon silent sobs racked his chest. He received a tissue from his wife and pressed it to his eyes.

"I'm sorry for your loss," said Chase, a little lamely, I thought. Then again, Chase is a good detective, always eager to catch his man, but he's not all that good at consoling people when a loved one has been killed.

"We'll do everything we can to catch the person who killed your father," said Odelia, and her words actually elicited a nod of appreciation from the stricken Royden. She's much better at the consoling part than Chase. Which is why she's a civilian consultant, of course. Uncle Alec added her to the team because people like her, and open up to her.

"Do you have any idea what your grandad wanted to talk to you about?" asked Chase.

Emma shook her head. "No idea. I tried calling him, but there was no reply."

"He was terrible with phones," Abisha explained. "Hated when people called him, and put off calling others as long as possible."

Which made me wonder how the man had built an empire, if he hated telephones so much. Then again, we all have our quirks, of course, and it was quickly becoming obvious to me that Rudyard van de Graaf had had plenty of them.

"Like I said, I thought it had something to do with Casey's wedding," said Emma.

"You think maybe he'd changed his mind about that?" asked Odelia.

"I doubt it," Abisha said. "In all the years I've known him, Rudyard has never changed his mind about anything. He considered it a sign of weakness to change his mind, even if it was obvious he was wrong."

"He could be very stubborn," Royden confirmed. "In fact when I talked to him about this wedding business he practically admitted that maybe he'd been too rash. But he couldn't back off now. It would be construed as weakness, and he couldn't have that."

"Even if it ruined his granddaughter's life?"

"Oh, Mrs. Kingsley," said Abisha. "Rudyard had no qualms about ruining other people's lives. In fact it was what he did best."

"Abisha!" said Royden sharply.

"It's true, isn't it? Your dad was a monster, Royden. He ruined your life, he ruined mine, and now he was going to ruin our children's lives as well." She shrugged. "In all honesty I'm not sure if this John Robie shouldn't receive a medal for what he did."

"My God, woman!" Royden cried.

"Isn't your father's death going to create even more trouble for the family?" asked Odelia. "I thought that if he died before Casey and Zalman were married he would dissolve the family holding and donate everything to his favorite charities?"

Royden and Abisha exchanged a look of concern. "We better talk to our lawyers," said Royden. "See if the old man's threats were for real."

Suddenly Emma rose to her feet. I noticed how her eyes were shooting fire... at her parents. "You two are horrible! Grandad is lying there, dead, and all you can do is call him a monster and worry about the money!"

And with these words, she stomped out of the room and slammed the door.

Abisha gave us a look of apology. "I'm sorry about that. Of all the grandkids Emma has always been closest to her grandad."

"At least one life he didn't ruin," Royden muttered, and took his wife's hand in his. Obviously he endorsed his wife's estimation of his late father, though perhaps not the fact that she'd voiced it in the presence of a cop.

CHAPTER 10

An officer entered the room, wanting to talk to Chase, and since the interview seemed to have come to an end anyway, the detecting pair walked out, followed by Dooley and yours truly, while Royden and Abisha stayed in the room, to talk through the consequences of Rudyard's sudden death.

"Yes, what is it?" asked Chase.

"Results from the neighborhood canvass, sir," said the officer. "One of the neighbors said she saw a cab drive up earlier. Rudyard was in the cab."

"What time was this?"

"Three-thirty, sir."

"So Rudyard was still alive at three-thirty, huh?"

"Looks that way, sir. The cab drove away, and Rudyard then went for a walk. The woman isn't sure when he came back. She said she has better things to do than to keep tabs on her neighbors all day."

Chase smiled. "She did a pretty good job. Thanks, Gerald."

"Yes, sir."

The cop hurried out, no doubt to talk to more nosy

parker neighbors, and Chase convened with Odelia. "So looks like Rudyard was still alive at three-thirty. According to the preliminary time window Abe gave us that would fix time of death between three-thirty and four."

"Emma said she arrived at four, so that makes sense."

"We need to find that cab driver. Find out what Rudyard was up to." He glanced to the entrance to the living room, where Royden now appeared, looking thoughtful. "Excuse me, sir, but do you have any idea why your father would take a cab? A neighbor says she saw a cab drive up around three-thirty, and deposit your dad at the front door."

Royden frowned at this, even as he rummaged around in his pocket, then extracted a pack of cigarettes. "That's odd," he said. "Dad almost never left the house. The only time he did was to go to the office, which he religiously did once a week."

"Maybe he went out to run an errand?"

"There's no need. We have people who do that for us. And why would he take a cab? We have a car at his disposal and a chauffeur. Though I have to tell you that Dad hated the fact that we still kept a chauffeur on the payroll. He thought it was an extravagance. But he certainly didn't tell me he was going somewhere."

"We'll talk to the cab driver," said Chase. "I'm sure he'll be able to tell us more."

Harriet and Brutus now came trudging down the stairs, looking very officious. "And?" I said. "Have you found the ghost of Rolf van de Graaf?"

Harriet gave me a supercilious look. "That's all just nonsense," she said.

"I know that, but I didn't know you knew."

"Oh, playing games, are we?" said Brutus, who looked as supercilious as his partner. "No need to be jealous, Max. Just because we are now the lead detectives in this case doesn't mean you should be sad."

"Or jealous," said Harriet.

"I'm not sad," I said, "or jealous. Just wondering if you're getting anywhere."

"Don't you worry about us," said Harriet. "We've almost cracked this case."

"How about you?" asked Brutus. "How far have you got in solving this murder?"

I shrugged. "It's early days."

"Typical amateur excuse," Harriet scoffed. "Let's go, Brutus. I feel Max's incompetence affecting my superior brain capacity already."

And then they were off, no doubt ready to name the killer at the first opportunity.

"Do you think Harriet and Brutus are ready to nab the killer, Max?" asked Dooley.

"Somehow I doubt it, Dooley," I said.

Just then, two more cats came trudging down those stairs. They were, of course, Henrietta and Bru.

"Where are the others?" asked Henrietta.

I gestured with my head in the direction Harriet and Brutus had left, and Henrietta gave me a keen look. "They didn't seem to take us seriously when we explained about the ghost of Rolf van de Graaf."

"Such a shame, right?"

She frowned, trying to determine whether I was serious or simply joshing her. Finally she decided on the former. "You know, one thing I didn't tell them is how the ghost travels from room to room, and manages to murder people without being seen."

"If it's a ghost, he'll simply travel through the walls," I pointed out.

"Regular ghosts, yes," said Henrietta. "But this ghost likes to do things a little differently. You see, when Rolf was still alive, he liked to use the secret passageways to move around this place, and since he died, he's kept up the habit."

"Secret passageways?" I asked. "What secret passageways?"

"Oh, hasn't anyone told you? This house is full of them. They will lead you all over the place, and even extend into the basement and as far up as the attic."

"And how do we get into those passageways?" I asked, thinking that this might be how John Robie had managed to get in and out of the house undetected.

"Follow me," said Henrietta, and turned on her heel.

"This is some good stuff," Bru assured us.

"Max, are you sure?" asked Dooley. "I don't like secret passageways."

"We're not actually going to explore them, Dooley," I said. "Just find out what they're all about, so we can tell Odelia."

Henrietta and Bru led us into the library, which looked like any library does: with racks and racks of books, and nice mahogany tables with those green reading lamps. There was even a window alcove, where plenty of reading could be done, nice and snug in the winter months, no doubt, with a big clunky radiator directly underneath your tush.

"Here we go," said Henrietta, as she placed a deft paw on one of the wooden panels that lined the walls. She gave it a little push, there was a click, and the panel swung open!

"Oh, my," said Dooley. "Now isn't this neat?"

"Go on," said Bru. "Take a peek."

And so Dooley and I set paw inside the space that lay behind the panel. And we'd only just done so when suddenly that panel swung closed behind us again, and we were plunged into darkness!

"Hey!" I yelled. "Open this door!"

"It's not really a door, Max," said Dooley. "It's a secret passage."

"Open the secret passage!" I cried.

But the only sound that reached my ears was a persistent giggling.

Looked like we'd been trapped!

CHAPTER 11

"Max?"

"Mh?"

"I don't think I like Henrietta and Bru very much."

"No, I don't like them either."

"And I don't like how they locked us up in the walls."

"There has to be a way out of here," I said. "If these passageways run all over the house, there will be many entrances and exits."

At least we were in the advantageous position that cats don't need much light to be able to see. Some light was filtering into the passageway through the paneling, and also from above.

"You know, Dooley, this might not be such a bad thing."

"It's not?"

"No, it stands to reason that the killer, whoever he is, used these very same passageways—or at least he did if he is the same person who stole that dagger last night. And judging from the fact that Mr. van de Graaf was killed with the Drossart Dagger, I think that's the only logical conclusion."

"So John Robie is the killer?"

"He must be. Where else did the killer get the dagger?"

"He could have borrowed it from John Robie?"

"You mean if John Robie isn't working alone?"

"Or if John Robie has a friend who asked if he could borrow a dagger? John Robie must have friends, too, Max, and if he's a good friend he wouldn't have said no if someone asked him for a favor. I mean, if you wanted to borrow my dagger, I'd say yes."

"And since John Robie is a criminal, he probably has criminal friends," I said, nodding. "It's possible, of course, though I'd replace 'borrow' with 'steal' in this case."

"Can we get out of here now? I don't like to be locked up in the walls of an old house."

"Yes, let's find a way out," I said. But I hadn't lied when I said that perhaps this was providential in the grand scheme of things. Now at least we could look into the possibility that John Robie had used these secret passageways to gain access to Rudyard's study.

Which of course begged the question once again how the man knew so much about the houses he targeted.

"Let's move up," I said. "And try to reach Rudyard van de Graaf's study. If we can manage that, we'll have proved that it's possible to gain access to the old man's apartment, and we'll be following in the killer's footsteps."

And so we moved off in the direction of where—if my sense of direction wasn't fooling me—the staircase was, and presumably also a way to reach the next floor.

I have to admit it wasn't at all a pleasant experience, since the people responsible for cleaning the place had clearly omitted to extend their services to these hidden spaces behind the walls. Then again, I don't think it was something that could be held against them. Like cleaners often don't sweep under the bed, they don't sweep behind the walls either—if they even knew these secret passageways existed.

We found a wooden staircase that did indeed match the one on the other side of the wall, and slowly made our way up.

"Max!" suddenly Dooley cried, and I looked over, ready to fight some formidable foe.

"What!" I cried, glancing in the direction he was looking.

"I think I saw a mouse!"

I relaxed. "I think there will probably be a lot of mice, Dooley, and other things, too."

"Not… the ghost of Rolf van de Graaf!"

"No, not him," I said reassuringly.

We trekked on, and I was just thinking that if I climbed these stairs every day for the next year or so, I'd be in the shape of my life, when I thought I heard voices. They came from the other side of the wall. And since curiosity is my second name, I put my ear to the wall and listened.

"We have to catch that killer first, Brutus!" Harriet was saying. "After all the fuss we made we can't afford to have Max catch him before we do."

"Maybe we shouldn't have said all those things," said Brutus. "Max is pretty smart. He'll probably figure it out before we do."

"No, no and no! This time we're going to catch the killer, if it kills us to do it."

"But I don't want to be killed, smoochie poo."

"It's just a manner of speech, wuggle bear."

"Oh. That's all right then."

"Okay, so think. Who would kill a rich person?"

"Um…"

"A not-so-rich person, of course!"

"Oh, right."

"And who's not rich in this house?"

"Um…"

"The staff!"

"Oh, yes. They're not rich, probably."

"So picture the scene: you work day and night for a very rich person, but you have to scrape and starve to get by."

"Do you think the van de Graafs don't pay them enough?"

"I'm sure of it. How else do you think they got so rich? Okay, so focus, sugar muffin."

"I'm focusing."

"So a staff member killed the old man."

"But I thought John Robie killed him?"

"They're one and the same! John Robie is a staff member, or how else did he know so much about this place? Or where to find the loot?"

"Okay."

"Ooh! I think I've got it, Brutus."

"You have? That was quick."

"It's easy, if you use your brain."

"So who did it?"

"The butler, Brutus. The butler did it!"

"Huh! Take that, Max!"

I retracted my ear from the wall with a smile. Harriet and Brutus might not believe in ghosts, but they did seem to believe in fairy tales.

"Did the butler do it, Max?" asked Dooley, who'd also listened in.

"He might have done it, if the van de Graafs had a butler. As it is, they don't. But I doubt that is going to stop Harriet from believing that he did do it."

"She's very competitive, isn't she?"

"She is. All the more reason for us to keep looking, and not to get sidetracked by Harriet's theories."

And we'd mounted another set of stairs when suddenly it

dawned on me that we could have yelled and asked Harriet and Brutus to let us out!

Duh! Okay, so maybe I'm not as smart as Harriet and Brutus seem to think I am!

We finally arrived at the top of the house, and now we needed to find a way to get out of our predicament, unless we accepted that we were going to take up permanent residence inside these walls. In which case we might need to start eating mice, which I really didn't want to do. I may not be a vegetarian, but I balk at gobbling down a mouse with hide and hair. So tacky. And clichéd, of course.

So we tapped the wall, and looked for an exit.

"Max, over here!" said Dooley. And as I joined him, I saw that he'd found a piece of wood paneling, just like the one downstairs in the library.

"There must be a way to trigger this from this side," I said. "How else do people move around the house?"

"I don't see a door handle, Max."

"No, that would be too easy."

And then suddenly I saw it: there was a sort of latch, also made of wood, engineered between two of the bricks that lined the panel. I pressed it, and presto! The panel clicked open about two inches. And then it was simply a matter of pushing it open further.

And lo and behold: we were in the same study where Rudyard had met his maker!

CHAPTER 12

When we entered that study, we surprised Odelia and Chase, who were looking around, and generally trying to work out what might have happened in that room. So when Dooley and I suddenly came popping out of the woodwork, so to speak, Odelia uttered a little scream of surprise, and even Chase lifted his right eyebrow about a tenth of an inch, which is probably about the extent he will ever go to to express surprise.

"Where did you guys come from?" asked Odelia.

"Henrietta and Bru locked us up in the walls," Dooley explained. "And Max thought it would be a good idea to see if we couldn't follow in John Robie's footsteps. And so we did." He shivered. "And we saw a mouse!"

Odelia turned to her husband. "Looks like there's a secret passageway that leads from downstairs all the way up to here."

They both opened the panel a little further still and glanced behind it.

"Well, I'll be damned," Chase grunted. He then turned to one of the techies in charge of dusting the room for prints

NIC SAINT

and collecting DNA and such and said, "You better check this out, buddy. Chances are the killer came in this way."

"I will, sir," said the techie, as he quickly inspected the secret hiding place.

"Good job, you guys," said Odelia, giving me a pat on the head and Dooley a tickle under the chin. "We were actually looking for you. Chase made an appointment with the lawyer handling Rudyard's estate."

"Could you maybe carry us?" I asked. I really didn't want to descend all those stairs again. Already my paws were killing me.

"Sure thing, sweetie," said Odelia, showing us she really is a human out of a thousand. And so she grabbed Dooley and Chase grabbed me and together we went down.

I don't know if I should have taken the fact that Chase—with his superior muscularity—chose to carry me while Odelia took the much lighter Dooley as a slur on my character, but in the end I decided not to. We had other, more important things to worry about.

Once downstairs, we met up with Harriet and Brutus, but when Odelia asked if they wanted to tag along and visit the lawyer, they both declined.

"We're on to the killer, Odelia," said Harriet, her eyes glittering. "I can't tell you too much about it right now, but I think we've got him cornered."

"That's great, honey," said Odelia, and we took our leave, leaving the Very Important Detective and her beefy sidekick behind.

Seymour Conlan, the van de Graaf lawyer, was a very nice man. He had a warm and pleasant personality, and his bedside manner was such that he would have made a great doctor. He stared at us from behind a desk that was much too large for him, his eyes twinkling as he first told us he couldn't possibly comment on matters of a confidential nature. But when Chase went through his usual routine of threatening to produce a warrant, he was only too pleased to spill the legal beans on Mr. van de Graaf.

"Rudyard made a very simple will. And he made it a long time ago. Everything goes to his son, Royden van de Graaf. And since the family business is comprised in a holding, it is that holding whose ownership will be transferred to Royden, wholly and complete."

"But what about the will that leaves his entire estate to charity?" asked Odelia.

Mr. Conlan smiled. "He told me about that. He wanted to induce his granddaughter to marry into the Mulhearn family, and to that end he made it out as if he would dissolve the holding and donate everything to charity. But as far as I know he never made good on that threat."

"So those were just words?"

"Those were mere words. A man in Rudyard's position, with the fortune his father and grandfather created, would never in his right mind undo the great work these men have done. And Rudyard, in spite of his age, was mentally as sharp as a tack. I don't think he ever even considered following through with the scenario as he'd outlined it to Casey."

"So an idle threat."

"Well, not entirely idle. He really wished for these two great families to come together, and he knew that if he didn't apply some pressure it would never happen." He spread his arms. "But I think he was also smart enough to realize that you simply cannot, in this day and age, make people fall in love. If it happens, it happens. If it doesn't?" He shrugged.

"So Casey's anxiety was for nothing," said Odelia softly.

"Yes, and I'm sure at some point he would have told her.

But then of course we'll never know." He eyed Chase keenly. "Have you any idea who might have killed him, detective?"

"We're following several promising lines of inquiry," said Chase, giving the lawyer the official police line.

The man smiled. "I've given you a peek into my inner kitchen, detective. Would you mind very much to give me a peek into yours?"

Chase returned the man's smile. "Let's just say that the John Robie angle seems to be the most promising one right now."

"John Robie, eh? How odd that a cat burglar would suddenly start murdering his victims. Cary Grant would never have agreed to play a vicious part like that."

"Cary Grant did play a murderer once," said Odelia. "In *Suspicion*. Though they changed the ending. In the original ending he actually ended up killing his wife."

The lawyer's smile widened. "And why did they change the ending, you think? Because Cary Grant would never be the killer. He simply wouldn't. The audience wouldn't have accepted it. Which makes it so hard for me to believe that John Robie would kill my client. But then I guess you know best."

Once we were outside again, Chase turned to Odelia. "What did you make of that?"

"About the will, you mean? I think Rudyard played a rotten trick on Casey, making her believe she had to marry the man he chose or else he'd ruin the family's future."

"Yes, but about that John Robie business."

"Don't listen to him, Chase. He's not a cop. You just trust your instincts."

"Well, my instincts are telling me that he's got a point. It makes no sense. First off, until now John Robie has only been active at night. And secondly, he's gone out of his way not to use violence. And now all of a sudden he shows up in the middle of the day, and kills the man he robbed the night before? I mean, why return to the house he burgled? And why carry that dagger?"

"Because he considers it a trophy and now takes it everywhere he goes?"

Chase gave her a look that spoke volumes about what he thought of Royden's theory.

"I don't think so," he said. He checked his watch. "We better go and talk to Sully Beblo."

"Who's he?"

"The cabbie who took Rudyard home this afternoon. Let's see what he has to say."

CHAPTER 13

Mr. Beblo, the cab driver, told us that he had indeed picked up Mr. van de Graaf at his home—the man had been waiting for him, clearly eager to get going—and had returned him safely home again afterward.

When Chase asked him where he'd taken the business tycoon, he said that the old man had told him to drive to Tallett, the well-known bespoke tailor in town, where he had proceeded to spend the better part of an hour. Asked about the purpose of his visit, Mr. van de Graaf had said that he wanted to have a new suit made for his birthday, which was coming up in just a few days.

"Sad business," said Sully Beblo, shaking his head. "A new suit made and now he's dead. I wonder what's going to happen to that suit." And the way he gave Chase a pointed look, told me that he was hoping the suit might go to the cab driver. "I mean, it would be such a waste to use an expensive suit for the funeral, wouldn't you say, Mr. Kingsley?"

Mr. Kingsley had too much common sense to answer that question, and had thanked the man for his cooperation.

. . .

PURRFECT THIEF

Our next port of call was Tallett, where Giuseppe Tallett himself—the bespoke tailor of which mention was made—greeted us with outstretched arms.

"Such a sad day for us, Detective Kingsley! One minute the man is being fitted for a suit, and next thing he's dead!" He slapped the palm of his hand with his fist. "Just like that! What was it, do you know? Heart attack? He was not a young man, was Mr. van de Graaf, but very nice—so very nice! He said not to spare any expense on the suit—picked our best design! If only all clients had such class—such style—such vision!"

"So you fitted him for a new suit?" asked Chase, glad to get a word in edgewise.

"Yes, a brand-new suit. A beautiful, *beautiful* suit! Wanna see?"

And without awaiting an answer, he disappeared into the back of his store, and moments later returned with what looked like a random patchwork of fine fabric, stitched together in a seemingly haphazard way.

"It doesn't look very nice," said Dooley.

"I think that's just the initial phase," I said.

"Look how beautiful!" said Mr. Tallett, who was a small man with a thin strip of a mustache.

"Very nice," said Odelia.

"Isn't it just, Mrs. Kingsley?" The energetic tailor was beaming with pride.

"So Rudyard van de Graaf was in here from what time?" asked Chase, determined not to get sidetracked.

"I think he came in about… two o'clock, maybe? And he was here for an hour or so. It usually takes longer to do a fitting, but he said he was in a hurry, so I did my very best to accommodate him."

"Was he a regular client of yours?"

"Oh, no! First time. Though of course I had heard of him.

It was such an honor to finally be selected to create a suit for a man of such stature."

"So he was in here from two until three," said Chase, jotting all this down in his little notebook. "And then he left. With the same cab that brought him."

"That's right. A little odd, I thought, for a man like Mr. van de Graaf not to use his own car and his own driver."

"Apparently he thought that having a chauffeur was an extravagance."

"Of course," said Mr. Tallett, sobered. "Even rich people have to economize. Except on suits!" he added.

"It must be nice to be a human and to be able to wear all these nice clothes," said Dooley as we wandered around the store and admired the costumes on display. "I wonder how I would look in a tux."

"Very dashing, probably," I said.

"I don't know, Max. A cat in a suit probably looks ridiculous, don't you think?"

"Oh, no, I think everyone looks great in a tux. Even a cat. Or a dog."

"I wish I could walk on my hind legs. I'd be a lot taller, and really fill out that tux."

I smiled at my friend. "They do make clothes for cats, you know."

"I know, but they make you look so ridiculous."

"Not all of them. I'll bet that if you asked Mr. Tallett to make you a bespoke suit, he'd really make you something gorgeous."

"You know, that's not such a bad idea, Max. I'll bet there's an untapped market in bespoke clothes for cats. Tailer-made, I mean. Not the stuff you can buy off the internet, which only looks good in the pictures."

Somehow I didn't think Mr. Tallett would enjoy making

clothes for cats. He seemed very much attached to creating suits for the well-to-do gentleman who could afford it.

"How much do you think it costs, to have a suit like this made?" asked Dooley as we had returned to the counter and were now studying the suit Rudyard had ordered.

"I'm not sure, Dooley, but I don't think they come cheap."

"Ten thousand, sir!" said Mr. Tallett. "That's how much Mr. Rudyard had agreed to pay. And now who's going to pay me for my time, for my design, for my materials!"

"I suggest you send the bill to Royden van de Graaf," said Chase. "I'm sure he'll be happy to pay."

"You really think so?" asked Giuseppe. He looked hopeful, yet doubtful.

"Just tell him that his dad had ordered himself a new suit, but passed away before he could pay you," Odelia suggested.

Giuseppe nodded fervently. "I will do that. I will do exactly that! I have bills to pay, too, you know. I'm very sorry that Mr. van de Graaf died, but business is business, after all."

Words the dead man would no doubt have wholeheartedly endorsed.

CHAPTER 14

And so the investigation took us right back to the house that Rolf van de Graaf built, since Chase and Odelia wanted to have another chat with Royden, now that it turned out that he was the main beneficiary of his father's will.

"It's usually the person who inherits who turns out to be the killer, isn't it, Max?" Dooley said in the car on the drive over.

"Often but not always," I said. "There are other motives apart from money to commit murder."

"Casey could have done it, if she felt that her grandfather was forcing her to marry a man she didn't love. Or Abisha. She probably wasn't happy that her daughter was unhappy."

"Let's just wait and see how the investigation proceeds," I suggested. "I have a feeling there is still a lot about the van de Graaf family that we don't know."

Royden was surprised to see us again so soon, though he shouldn't have been. The police have a habit of circling back again and again to the same people, until they've finally homed in on the person of interest. And right now he was that person of interest.

"So I stand to inherit the lot? Now that is something I didn't know," said Royden.

Once again we were in the living room, only this time it was only Royden. Abisha was busy in the kitchen, handling some contretemps with the cook, apparently.

"Your dad didn't confide in you about his succession?" asked Chase, who clearly didn't give much credence to Royden's statement.

"Well, of course I always thought I'd inherit, but lately he'd begun to harp on this wedding business so much that I really believed he must have made a new will favoring his charities, and leaving the family out in the cold."

"Who else was aware of the contents of his will?" asked Chase.

"Well, my wife, of course, and one or two people who run the holding for us. Money managers. They're professionals, and know what they're doing. It seemed only fair that they would be kept informed about potential changes."

"And it now looks as if there won't be any changes."

"No, it certainly looks that way. And I won't conceal the fact that I'm much relieved. You hear so many horror stories about families being ripped apart, and the family fortune squandered by inheritance disputes, that frankly I was preparing myself for the worst."

"Were you planning on contesting the will if it turned out that your father had favored those charities?"

"I would certainly have consulted with our lawyers," Royden confirmed. "The van de Graaf holding has been around for decades, detective, and provides employment to a lot of people. It's only prudent that I shouldn't idly stand by and watch it all go down the drain, as a consequence of an old man's whim."

"Of course," said Chase.

"You must be very happy that Casey is free to marry her boyfriend now," said Odelia.

"Oh, yes," said the man, dragging his fingers through his graying mane. Then he frowned. "These questions… surely you're not suggesting that I had something to do with my father's murder, are you? Because I can assure you that I would never—"

"Remind us again where you were at four o'clock, sir?" Chase interrupted him.

"I already told you. I was on my way home from the office. The helicopter ride only takes forty-five minutes. I left there at three, and arrived here just in time for Emma to…" He swallowed. "To come screaming down the stairs, telling us she'd found Dad… dead."

It all sounded very plausible, and of course we could always ask the helicopter pilot.

Our next port of call was the kitchen, since that was where we could find Abisha. Only by the time we arrived she had already left. But since Dooley and I were getting seriously peckish again, we were only too glad to see two nice big bowls of kibble, and since there was no one around, we both happily dug in.

"Terrible business, that," said the cook, wiping her hands on her apron. "Mr. Rudyard was a difficult man to please, but murder!"

"He was difficult, you say?" asked Chase.

"Oh, extremely difficult. Whatever I cooked, he always had some comment to make. If I cooked him potatoes he said he hated potatoes and preferred rice. If I cooked him rice he said he hated rice and preferred potatoes. When I served him meat he said he wanted vegetarian food and when I cooked vegetarian he said no meal was complete without meat! There was simply no pleasing the man. Oh, no, he was certainly very difficult."

"This is some good stuff, Max," said Dooley between two bites.

"Yeah, maybe we should tell Odelia to ask the cook what it is."

"Good idea."

"Do you know that he hired a caterer for his birthday?" the cook went on. "A caterer, if you please! As if my cooking wasn't good enough for him." She shook her head. "I had a good mind to quit when they told me. And then when the caterer arrived and started bossing us all around as if he owned the place? I came this close to throwing in the towel. This close." She was holding her thumb and index finger very close together indeed. "Especially when you consider that Mr. Guy and Miss Emma have a lot of history."

"Mr. Guy is the caterer?" asked Odelia.

The cook nodded. "Guy Batozy. He has a big fancy restaurant in town. Him and Miss Emma used to date, you see, until they didn't."

"And why was that?"

"I'm sure I don't know. They don't tell me anything around here. Except when they don't like my food. Though I guess now that Mr. Rudyard is dead the big birthday do will be off. Now there's a silver lining for you."

"So about this afternoon, Mrs…"

"Adler. Eunice Adler. And it's Miss. I never married. Never found the right man. It's tough to combine a household with my position here, you see. Plenty of work to do."

"I can imagine," said Odelia with a smile.

"So about this afternoon, Miss Adler," Chase continued, trying to keep the conversation on track and not skipping around like a rubber ball. "Did you notice anything unusual? Strangers hanging around the house?"

"No strangers," said Eunice decidedly. "If I had seen anyone acting suspicious, I would have kicked them out. You might think that a big place like this would have security people posted everywhere, but no. Nothing! Mr. Rudyard was dead set against it. When you lock a place down, you lock yourself in, he always said, so no security. Though he did allow CCTV, but only last year, and only after Mr. Royden insisted."

"Unfortunately the CCTV wasn't set to record," said Chase. "And since it looks as if nobody actually watches the feed, those cameras might as well not have been there."

"Typical," Eunice snorted. "Now if there's nothing else, I have to get back to my cooking. Mr. Rudyard might be dead, but the rest of the family isn't, and they'll be hungry."

Just as I had been. But as I now sat licking my lips, enjoying the aftermath of a good meal, I saw how Henrietta and Bur came tripping into the kitchen. They seemed surprised to see us, and even more surprised to find their bowls completely devoid of kibble.

"Who ate our food?" asked Henrietta, looking stunned. "Did you two eat our food?" she asked, addressing me.

I shrugged as I walked past, following Chase and Odelia out of the kitchen. "I think it was probably the ghost of Rolf van de Graaf," I said. "Even ghosts get hungry, you know."

I ignored her fiery look in my direction, and Bru's low growl, and walked out.

And as we arrived in the corridor, suddenly I became aware of a sort of plaintive mewling. It was coming from behind the wall. Odelia must have heard it too, for immediately she started tapping the wall. The mewling intensified both in volume and pitch, and before long Royden showed up.

"I think one of the cats got stuck in the wall again," he said. He pressed the corner of one of the panels, and it promptly swung open, revealing none other than Harriet and Brutus!

"They locked us in!" Harriet cried. "Those brutes lured us into the wall and locked us in!"

"They did the same with us," said Dooley.

"Of all the mean, horrible, dirty, rotten tricks!"

"I'm going to get them for this," Brutus growled, looking not too well pleased.

"Let's get them later, though," I said. "Right now is not the time to confront them."

"Oh, and why is that, pray tell?" asked Harriet.

"Because we just ate all of their kibble," said Dooley.

This caused a slow grin to spread across our friends' faces, and as we followed Odelia and Chase out of the house and into the car, I think we all felt a little better knowing that at least we got some of our own back.

CHAPTER 15

We were in the car heading home when a call came in on Chase's mobile. It was Uncle Alec. Chase put his phone on speaker so we could all enjoy listening to the Chief's voice.

"Better get over to Rutherford Street 51, buddy."

"Why? What's at Rutherford Street 51?"

"Better ask who. Emma van de Graaf, that's who."

"Casey's sister?"

"Her fingerprints were found on the murder weapon."

"Uh-oh."

"Oh, and one other thing. Forensics didn't find a phone in Rudyard's possession. So if she got a call from him, it's very well possible that she made that call herself. To give herself a reason to drive over there—if she even got a call at all."

"No, but I saw the message," said Odelia, leaning in over Chase's phone, which was in its holder, as per traffic safety regulations. "She really did get a message."

"Then she must have sent that message to herself, using a prepaid mobile phone. Better go over there now, and find out what's going on."

"Will do, Chief," said Chase, and disconnected. He

glanced over to Odelia. "Well, that puts a completely different spin on things."

"It does, indeed."

Harriet, sitting in the backseat along with the rest of us, looked glum. "And here I thought that the butler had done it," she muttered.

"The van de Graafs have no butler," I pointed out. "But they do have a cook and a gardener and a chauffeur. And probably maids, too."

"Oh, don't rub it in, Max," said Harriet, then addressed Odelia. "Can you drop us off at the house, please? We're both very hungry and we need to think."

"Of course," said Odelia, and transferred the message to her husband.

"Think about what?" asked Dooley.

"Think about the case!" Harriet snapped. "In case you didn't know, detectives are always thinking about the case, Dooley."

"I thought detectives collected clues and talked to suspects," he said.

"And what do you know about the way a real detective operates?" asked Harriet. "A real detective doesn't need clues or suspects, Dooley. They don't inspect cigar ash or study fingerprints with a magnifying glass or examine footprints left in the flowerbeds. All a real detective needs is this." She tapped her head.

"Fur?" Dooley suggested.

"Little gray cells!"

"Oh, right."

"So I'm going home, and I'm going to think. And by the time you're all finished running around like a bunch of headless chickens, I will have solved this case."

"That's great, Harriet," said Dooley.

"VI Harriet to you, Dooley," she said, then lapsed into

silence, no doubt whipping those little gray cells of hers into a frenzy of activity.

Once Harriet and Brutus had been dropped off at the house, Chase set a course for Rutherford Street 51, and we were in luck, as Emma was in, and so was her boyfriend, one Vincent Rebela, schoolteacher by profession.

"Yes, what is it?" asked Emma once we'd all taken a seat in her cozy living room. Vincent had on an apron and had been busy stirring the pots, but now also joined us.

"We need to ask you a few more questions, Emma," said Odelia.

"Of course."

"Is this about Rudyard's death?" asked Vincent. He was a good-looking young man, with a boyish countenance and floppy brown hair. All in all I could totally see him and Emma being perfectly happy together, in their tastefully decorated apartment.

"Yes, I'm afraid so."

"The dagger that was used to kill your grandfather," Chase began, causing Emma to wince, "contained one set of fingerprints."

"Yes?"

"Yours, Emma."

The girl looked taken aback. "What?!"

"How do you explain that?"

"I don't understand how…"

"Did you touch the dagger when you found your grandfather?"

"No, I didn't touch anything. I just ran out of that room and down the stairs. I was so shocked I couldn't think straight."

"So how do you explain the fact that your fingerprints were on the dagger?"

"Now hold on a moment," said her boyfriend, scooting

forward on the couch. "How can you be so sure those are Emma's fingerprints? As far as I know she's never been fingerprinted in her life, so maybe you're confusing her with someone else."

"Her fingerprints were in the system, actually," said Chase. "She was arrested once at a protest march against political oppression in Venezuela."

"I remember," said Emma, nodding. "But that was years ago. I was a teenager."

"That still doesn't change the fact that your fingerprints were found on the murder weapon, Emma," Chase insisted.

"Look, I really have no idea how that happened," Emma said, shaking her head dismally.

"I'm sure there must be some mistake," said Vincent. "Some kind of mix-up in your database."

"No mix-up. No mistake."

"I think we better get you a lawyer, honey," said Vincent quietly, putting an arm around his girlfriend's shoulder. "You don't have to say anything more."

"Your boyfriend is right, Emma," said Chase. "You don't have to say anything if you don't want to, but it's going to look awfully suspicious if you go down that route."

"I didn't kill my grandfather, if that's what you mean!" she said, and suddenly there was some steel in her voice. She might look like a sweet girl, but she had fire in her soul.

"We're not saying you killed your grandpa," said Odelia gently. "But you have to understand that we can't ignore this."

Emma nodded, then said, "I think I'm done with this interview. I'm going to contact a lawyer, and next time you want to talk to me, you better do it through them."

"There's one other thing we wanted to talk to you about," said Odelia.

"What?" said Emma reluctantly.

"You dated a man named Guy Batozy for a while?"

"That's private," she said immediately.

"I just—"

"I'm sorry, Mrs. Kingsley, but like I said, I'm done talking to you. Please leave."

And just when things looked pretty bleak, I noticed a bowl of kibble in the kitchen. I always notice bowls of kibble in kitchens, wherever I am. And where there is kibble, there is a cat. So naturally I went in search of this cat, and found her sleeping on a chair in the kitchen.

"Hey, there," I said.

"Oh, hi," said the cat, yawning widely and looking at me a little sleepily.

"My name is Max," I said. "What's yours?"

"Minnie," said the cat, who was of the smallish gray variety, not unlike Dooley, but a female of the species.

"Hey, Minnie. I hope I didn't wake you."

"You did, but that's okay. Are you a friend of Emma's?"

"Yeah, a great friend."

"That's nice," she said with a smile. "Any friend of Emma's is a friend of mine."

Dooley had now also joined us, and seemed immediately transported to another world when he spotted Minnie. "H-hi," he said haltingly. "M-m-my name is D-d-d-dooley."

"Hi, Dooley,'" she said. "Do you always stutter like that?"

"N-no," said Dooley. "Only when I meet a b-b-b-beautiful c-c-cat like y-y-you."

"Why, thanks, Dooley. That's very sweet of you to say."

"So Minnie," I said, wanting to get some information before Emma kicked us out, "your human, does she own a nice-looking dagger? It's called the Drossart Dagger and it's got all these gems on the hilt."

"Oh, I saw that," said Minnie. "Emma showed it to me last night. It's beautiful, isn't it?"

"It is," I agreed. "Where did she buy it?"

"She didn't buy it, silly. She stole it."

Now both Dooley and myself were quiet. Finally I managed to ask, "Stole it?"

"Of course. Emma and Vincent go out from time to time to steal stuff. They love it. You should see the kinds of things they bring home. One night she even brought me a portrait of a cat—it looked just like me! She said it was painted by a man named Picasso."

"Is your human the c-c-cat burglar?" asked Dooley, emerging from his momentary stupor.

"She is, and a very good one, too. But of course she used to do a lot of gymnastics when she was young, so she's very limber. And Vince is always there to help her get in and out of places. It's a great little hobby, don't you think?"

"It is," I said, feeling a little feverish all of a sudden. "A very nice little hobby."

CHAPTER 16

Chase has always been a fast worker, but today he was even quicker off the mark than usual. The moment Emma had kicked us out, and I'd recounted our recent conversation with Minnie, Odelia immediately told Chase, and moments later the cop was on the phone with the Chief to arrange a warrant.

And so we stood dawdling on the sidewalk for just a little while, watching the curtains move of the apartment where Emma and Vincent were presumably getting a little hot under their collar right now, and when the call came that the warrant had been granted, and three cop cars arrived, Chase pounded that door with his fist once more.

This time Emma didn't look as complacent as she had before, especially when a steady stream of boys and girls in blue poured into the apartment she shared with her boyfriend.

It didn't take them long to find what they were looking for, and so between the time that Emma had asked us to kindly leave, and the time we sat in that same living room, a stack of stolen goods piled high on the coffee table, the tables had been turned.

All around us, the search continued, but the pile of valuables was enough to elicit from Chase the following words: "So John Robie, huh? How did you manage to get into so many places undetected, Emma? And how the hell did you get access to the alarm codes?"

Emma shrugged. She looked a lot less indignant now that she'd been caught red-handed. Minnie was sitting in her lap, unaware of the consequences of her words.

"It's not that hard when your parents are friends with these people, detective. I've been in and out of those places all my life, and they hold no secrets for me."

"But why? I'm guessing you don't need the money."

"No, I don't," said Emma, looking up. There was a certain defiance in her eyes, as if she was convinced that what she'd done was right.

"So why do it? Why risk everything? For the kick?"

"No, I didn't do it just for kicks," said Emma. She looked down again. "You wouldn't understand," she said softly.

"Try me. For instance, why rob your own grandfather? Why take the Drossart Dagger?"

"Do you know the history of the Drossart Dagger, detective?" asked Emma.

"You don't have to explain, sweetheart," said Vincent.

"But I want to explain. I want to tell them why we did it." She took out her phone and placed it on the table. "This is the Drossart Dagger," she said, pushing the phone across the table in Chase's direction.

He took it and glanced at the page Emma had called up. "Yeah, I heard about the Nazi link. The Chief mentioned something about that."

"What he probably didn't mention was how my grandfather came to be in the possession of the dagger," said the young woman.

"Don't tell me your grandfather was a Nazi?"

"No, he wasn't, but he was friends with one. A very nasty character named Arnolf Zubeck. The Drossart Dagger used to belong to a Jewish family, descendants of Otto Drossart, the original owner of the dagger. The family had all of their possessions stolen by the Nazis, and the dagger ended up in the possession of Arnolf Zubeck, a war criminal. After the war, he escaped to the US, changed his name to Arnold Beck, and since he was friends with my great-grandfather before the war, they ended up rekindling their friendship."

"What happened to the Drossart family?"

"Most of them died in the camps. There are still some family members left, though. I've actually been in touch with some of Otto Drossart's descendants."

"So Zubeck was a war criminal, huh?"

Emma nodded. "Of the worst kind. But that didn't seem to matter to my great-grandfather, or Grandpa. On the contrary. They helped Zubeck with his documents, his new identity, helped him settle into his new life. As a reward, Zubeck gave them the Drossart Dagger."

"So maybe your grandpa and great-grandfather weren't aware of its history?"

"Oh, they most certainly were. They knew all about it, but instead of returning it to the Drossart family, they decided to keep it. Grandpa kept it in his so-called treasure chest, where he admired it every day, sipping from a whiskey and smoking a cigar." It was clear from the inflection of her voice and her expression what she thought of her grandfather's habit. "And it wasn't just the Drossart Dagger. Some of the most expensive and rare pieces of his collection also used to belong to Zubeck, who left them to him when he died."

"So stolen Nazi art, huh?"

Emma nodded. "The only reason I stole the dagger, and the other stuff, was so I could return it to the families it was stolen from."

"Emma and I are members of the Restitution Project," Vincent explained. "We hunt around for stolen treasure, and try and have it restored to the rightful owners."

"By stealing it?"

Vincent shrugged. "Unfortunately some of the people who own it are less than scrupulous people, and not inclined to do the right thing."

"So you give them a helping hand."

"We do what must be done," said Emma sternly. There was a holy fire in her eyes now, and it was clear she wholeheartedly believed in her cause.

"And what about the other stuff you stole?"

"I can assure you that we didn't steal anything, detective. All the stuff we took was stolen in the first place, and the people I took it from had no business owning it. But they're very good at hiding these valuable objects in their possession. And because of my unique position as a van de Graaf, I was privileged to be allowed to see them. Like my grandfather's dagger. He was adamant that no one should find out that he had it. But once I knew, I couldn't sit idly by and let him cherish his stolen goods, now could I?"

"Okay, so what I don't understand is why you returned with the dagger and murdered him," said Chase.

Emma looked up with a jerk. "What?"

"I can understand why you would want to kill him—because he was conspiring with Nazis and harboring stolen goods, and you clearly feel very strongly about these things. But why kill him with his own dagger and then leave it behind? You should have known we'd find your fingerprints on the weapon."

"But... I didn't kill my grandfather, detective. Of course I didn't. I may not have liked the fact that he was friends with Nazis, and that he kept stolen art, but I didn't kill him."

"Emma would never do such a thing," Vincent said.

Chase turned to him. "So how about you, Vince? You were there when your girlfriend burgled these places, weren't you? What role did you play?"

"I mainly stood watch," said Vincent reluctantly. "And also I supplied the material. The clothes, ropes, pulleys and such. We're both members of a mountaineering club, and climbing is a passion we share."

"But it was my idea, detective," said Emma. "It was me who pulled Vincent into this, not the other way around."

"How well did you get along with Emma's grandfather, Vincent?" asked Chase.

"I got on with him reasonably well, I suppose," said Vincent, a little guardedly.

"So was it you who returned this afternoon and planted that dagger into his heart?"

"No, of course not!" said Vincent, taken aback by this accusation.

"Look, we may be thieves," said Emma, "but we're not murderers. All we tried to do was to make things right. These people, my parents' friends, they had no right having this stuff hanging on their walls, or locked up in their vaults, or even dangling from their ears and necks to impress their friends. But no one was doing anything about it. So we decided that the only way to do right by the victims was simply to take it. But murder? Never."

"We don't believe in violence," Vincent said.

"All right," said Chase, "so how do you explain that the dagger that you admittedly stole ended up in the chest of your grandfather?"

Emma and Vincent shared a look. "We did have a break-in, didn't we?" said Emma hesitantly.

"Emma thinks that someone broke into the apartment," Vincent explained, "but nothing was taken, so we didn't report it."

"Nothing was stolen? So how do you know there was a break-in?" asked Odelia.

"Things were out of place," said Emma. "I'm very nitpicky about the way I organize my stuff. My kitchen cabinets, for instance. I have an exact place where I like to put my cups, my glasses, my plates, cutlery… And when I came home today, I noticed how things had been moved. As if someone had been rifling through our stuff." She frowned and pointed to a painting that hung over the mantelpiece. "That painting was crooked, for instance. And also, in the bathroom the door of the cabinet over the sink was ajar. I always close it."

"Did you notice these things, too, Vince?" asked Odelia.

Vincent seemed to waver, but then decided that telling the truth was his best bet. "Honestly? No, I didn't. But then I'm not as meticulous as Em."

"But nothing was stolen as far as you know?"

"I don't think so," said Emma.

"How did the thieves get into your apartment, you think?" asked Chase. It was clear that he didn't give much credence to this story.

"I'm not sure," Emma admitted.

"The lock was forced? Window broken?"

"No, everything looked fine—I checked."

"So what are you saying—the burglar had a key?"

Emma gave him an angry look. "I know that someone was in here. I could feel it."

"And they're the ones that stole the dagger and killed your grandfather?"

She nodded, but seemed to realize how thin her story sounded. "Look, all I can say is that I would never, ever hurt my grandfather—or anyone, for that matter."

"Even if they hobnob with Nazis and boast about the wealth they built on the heads of suffering families?"

She pressed her lips together, and Vincent said, "I think we better contact that lawyer now, detective, since it's obvious that you don't believe a word we say."

"Are you surprised, Vincent?"

He glanced to his girlfriend, then repeated, "I want to talk to a lawyer now."

"One more question," said Odelia, even as Emma shook her head in a clear sign that she'd had enough. "Did you tell anyone else about the Drossart Dagger or the fact that you are John Robie?"

"No, I didn't," said Emma.

"Best not to answer any more questions," Vincent said softly as he took Emma's hand.

"So no one knew that you had the dagger?"

Emma shook her head. "No one."

"Em," said Vincent emphatically. "No more."

CHAPTER 17

We were just exiting the house, with Emma and Vincent now in handcuffs and being led into a squad car, when a red Mini Cooper came zooming up at great speed, screeched to a halt, and Casey hurried out.

"Emma!" she cried after her sister. "Em!"

But the car carrying her sister off was already pulling away from the curb, and all Casey could do was stare at her sister, who gave her a sad glance, then looked away.

"What's going on!" Casey demanded. "Why did you take my sister?"

"Calm down, Casey," said Odelia, placing both hands on the woman's arms. But Casey shrugged them off.

"I demand to know what's happening!" she said.

"Emma has been arrested for burglary," said Odelia.

"What?!"

"She confessed, Casey. She is John Robie—she and Vincent. We found the stuff that was stolen in their apartment—all of it."

"But that's not possible! Not Em…"

"It's true, I'm afraid. And we also have a strong suspicion that she killed your grandfather."

"No!"

"The dagger that was used carried only one set of fingerprints and those were hers. And also, she was the one who stole the dagger last night."

"But she would never do that. Never. I know my sister, Odelia. She's not a killer."

"But you do believe that she's the cat burglar?"

Casey reluctantly nodded. "Em has been in a very weird place lately. Ever since she broke up with Guy, she hasn't been feeling well. We all hoped that now that she was with Vincent she'd start to feel better, but clearly her head is still not in the right place."

"Guy? Guy Batozy?"

"Yes. They used to date for a while, but things ended badly, and she broke up with him. They were going to get married at some point, but I never thought that was in the cards."

"Why not? Didn't they get along?"

"You'll have to ask Em for the details, but no, they clearly weren't right for each other."

"And so you think this breakup led to her going down the wrong path?"

"I'm not a psychologist, but I think it may have had something to do with it. She wasn't like this before. And whatever you say, I can't believe that she would murder our grandad. That's simply not possible."

"Did she ever talk to you about this John Robie business?"

"No, she didn't. Ever since she moved out we haven't been as close as we used to be. But I did have the impression she was involved in something that was having a bad influence on her. She kept going on and on about war crimes and the Nazis and stolen art. I thought it was because of Vincent. He teaches history, you see, and I thought he was filling her head with all kinds of nonsense."

"She wasn't into this stuff before?"

"No, of course not. As a kid she was into gymnastics and then horses for a while. She was going to become a professional jockey, we all thought, but then she met Guy and those plans went out the window. Instead the two of them were going to build a chain of restaurants. And then she met Vincent and suddenly it's all about Nazis and art. It's crazy."

"I know," said Odelia commiseratingly.

"I better tell Mom and Dad. They need to arrange a lawyer for Em." And taking out her phone, she got back into her car.

Minnie had come out of the house, and was looking a little curious.

"What's going on?" she asked. "What is all the fuss about?"

"I'm afraid your humans have been arrested," I told her.

"Yeah, they've been very bad," Dooley chimed in. He still seemed a little tongue-tied around Minnie but was improving with leaps and bounds. He could string a full sentence together already without a single stutter.

"Arrested? But why?"

"Well, you saw that pile of stolen loot, right?" I asked.

"All those nice things they collected? Sure."

"None of those things belonged to them. They stole them from other people. And that kind of stuff is usually frowned upon."

"They did it for a good cause, though," said Dooley. "They stole from thieves to return the stolen stuff to the rightful owners."

"Oh, so that's a good thing, right?"

"A very good thing," I said. "Only the law has a different opinion. They frown on that kind of behavior."

"So… how long are they going to be arrested for?"

"I'm not sure," I said. "They'll probably be bailed out, though, so they might be home in a couple of days."

"A couple of days! But who's going to feed me? Who's going to clean out my litter box?"

"Um…" I said. Now here was a contingency I hadn't really taken into consideration and neither, I assumed, had Odelia or Chase.

"Odelia?" asked Dooley immediately. "Can Minnie come and stay with us, please? She doesn't have her humans with her anymore."

"Oh, sure," said Odelia. "Though maybe her sister will want to take her—or Emma's mom and dad."

"Don't you think she'll be better off with us?" asked Dooley. "You're so good with cats, Odelia. It will be a great experience for her."

"Well…" said Odelia, glancing down to Minnie.

Just then, Casey exited her car again. "Mom and Dad are arranging Em's lawyer. So when do you think she'll be out?"

"I'm not sure," said Odelia. "First she and Vincent will be arraigned, and that's when the judge will decide whether they're eligible for bail."

"When is this arraignment?"

"Usually very quickly after an arrest. A matter of days."

"Great," said Casey curtly. She now stooped down, and scooped up Minnie. "Let's take you home, babes," she said. And before Dooley could react, she had deposited the small gray cat into her car and was driving off.

"Minnie!" said Dooley. "Where is she going?"

"Home with Casey," said Odelia, who seemed relieved. It's probably not such a good idea to take the cat of the person you just arrested home with you. And I'm sure Chase would have had a few things to say about it as well.

"You'll see Minnie again soon," I told Dooley, patting him on the back in a gesture of consolation. Or not.

CHAPTER 18

Odelia decided that a visit to Emma's now infamous ex-boyfriend was in order, to follow up on Emma's arrest. The restaurant Guy Batozy owned was located in the heart of town, and was one of the more expensive places where one could wine and dine. It wasn't the kind of eatery where Odelia and Chase had ever put their feet under the table, but then again, a policeman's salary, even when added to that of a reporter, doesn't stretch that far. Also, I don't think they're into five-star meals at fancy restaurants. They're more down-to-earth people, and seem to prefer a nice home-cooked meal at most times.

Mr. Batozy himself was a very friendly restaurateur, who was more than happy to offer us some of his no doubt valuable time.

"Yeah, I used to date Emma," he said once we'd taken place around a table at the back. He had opted for a seat where he could still have an overview of the place, and keep an eye both on his customers and his personnel. "Two years ago now, I think? Though we're still on good terms. They asked me to do the catering for the old man's birthday, so I think that says enough."

"You've heard about what happened to Rudyard van de Graaf?" asked Chase.

"Yeah, terrible business. I hope you catch the bastard who did this. If a person can't even feel safe in his own home…"

"Where were you, by the way, yesterday afternoon at four, Mr. Batozy?"

"Right here. You can ask anyone. The place was packed. I mainly worked the kitchen, jumping in for one of our sous-chefs who didn't show up. Again, I might add."

"So can you tell us a little bit more about your relationship with Emma?" asked Odelia.

"Not much to tell, I'm afraid. We went out a couple of times, then dated for a while, but ultimately things didn't work out between us."

"So she broke up with you."

"Actually I broke up with her. I found her too needy for my taste. Too young and immature. Em still has a lot of growing up to do. She sometimes acts more like a child than a grown woman. Spoiled, you know. Always wanting to have her way, and when things go wrong, she throws a tantrum. After a while it just became too much for me, so I called it quits."

"That's odd," said Chase. "Cause we heard a different story."

"Oh?"

"That she broke up with you."

"Of course she would say that. Save face in front of her friends and family. Anyway, that's all ancient history." He frowned. "I'm sorry, but what has this got to do with those burglaries?"

"Just collecting some background information," said

Chase noncommittally. "Trying to get a picture of the van de Graaf family."

Guy grinned. "You'll have your work cut out for you. Now there's a family with plenty of skeletons in their closet."

"Can you explain that?"

"Well, just look at them. You've got your crusty old patriarch, hated by all—"

"Rudyard was hated by all?"

"Sure. Royden hated his dad because he was always on his case. Calling him a weakling who was a disgrace to the good family name. Then there's Abisha, who wasn't good enough to marry a van de Graaf, according to Rudyard. And of course there's Royce."

"Royce?"

"Emma and Casey's older brother."

"What's wrong with him?"

"Nothing, except that he's gay, and Rudyard didn't like that. In fact if he'd had his way, he would have kicked him out of the family. But of course Royden and Abisha wouldn't have that. It created a lot of tension."

Chase cut a quick glance to Odelia, as if to say: did you get all that? Odelia nodded. She got all that, all right. Loud and clear.

"Where can we find this Royce?"

"He's married now, and lives with his husband."

"His husband?"

"That's right. Another fact that Rudyard hated about him: he didn't marry a nice girl and pretend he wasn't gay. No, he had to go and marry a man and declare to all the world that the heir to the van de Graaf millions likes men. Suffice it to say the old man was furious. He refused to attend the wedding, and decided to have nothing more to do with Royce. In fact I don't think he ever spoke to him again."

"Nice family," said Chase wryly.

"Yeah, so you'll understand why I wasn't exactly bowled over when my relationship with Em ended. Normally you'd think marrying into a family like the van de Graafs is any man's dream come true. But frankly they shocked me more than once. A viper's nest in the truest sense of the word. Nuts?" He slid a bowl of nuts in the cop's direction, and the cop gratefully grabbed a handful. I guess he was starting to get a little peckish. And of course there were all those delicious smells wafting in from the kitchen, which was located right next to us. That swinging door swung open and closed all the time, and each time it sent those olfactory molecules drifting in our direction.

Sweet agony!

"Do you think maybe we can go and visit Minnie?" asked Dooley now, when there was a short lull in the conversation.

"I doubt it, Dooley," I said. "I had the impression that Casey isn't very happy with us right now, after Odelia and Chase arrested her sister."

"But I thought she liked us so much."

"She did, but once you start accusing people's relatives of murder, those warm feelings they harbor are quickly replaced with something more akin to resentment."

"Pity."

"Okay," said Chase, "I think that's all for now. Unless you can think of something else that might help us?"

"Nothing springs to mind," said the restaurateur. "Except…"

"Yes?"

"Well, the old man was killed with his own dagger, right?"

"How did you know?"

"News travels fast in this town, detective."

"Okay, so?"

"He showed it to me once."

"He showed you the dagger?"

"Yeah, the old boy had taken a real liking to me. I think he thought I might be a good substitute for Royce. He said I had a good head for business, unlike the rest of his worthless offspring. Anyway, he said he had something special to show me, and so he led me into his treasure room. And what a treasure it was. But his pride and joy was that dagger. He said he could look at that thing for hours. Which made me wonder, you know."

"Wonder what?"

"How can a man prefer a stupid old dagger over his own flesh and blood? He seemed to like that thing more than he did his son or grandkids. But anyway, he said something then that I've always remembered. He said that if something ever happened to him, the police shouldn't look for a stranger, but to one of his so-called nearest and dearest." He shook his head. "Can you imagine the mind of a man who thinks like that?"

Chase and Odelia got up and shook the restaurateur's hand, thanking him for his time. In return he offered them his card and a ten-percent discount on their next visit.

A man might be a witness in a murder investigation, but above all, he's still a businessman, and cops have to eat, too, right?

CHAPTER 19

It had been a long day, but we were finally home again. And so after spending some quality time with my bowl of kibble, I settled down on the couch, ready to catch up on my naptime. Unfortunately Chase and Odelia decided to talk about the case, and so instead of cooking dinner, they took a seat right next to me and Dooley, and talked turkey instead.

"So do you think Emma is our killer?" asked Chase. He's always interested to hear Odelia's opinion, whom he considers an ace sleuth, even though she's actually an ace reporter. The two professions do overlap, of course.

"I don't know," said Odelia. "She doesn't strike me as the murdering type."

"Murderers don't have a type, babe. Anyone can be a killer."

"Just like anyone can cook," said Dooley, courtesy of *Ratatouille*.

"And how else do you explain the dagger?" Chase asked.

"It could have been stolen from her apartment," said Odelia, "just like she said."

"I don't believe that story about a break-in for even one second," said Chase. "If anyone had broken in, they would have taken everything. Those two had stuff stacked up in their apartment worth hundreds of thousands or maybe even millions. So why would any self-respecting thief break in and then only grab that dagger? And leave no fingerprints but perfectly preserve Emma's prints? That makes no sense at all."

"Yeah, I know. It is a very fishy story. Especially since Vincent admitted he hadn't noticed any signs of a break-in himself."

"But what I don't understand is why she would be stupid enough to kill her grandfather with his own dagger, and forget to wipe her prints? Unless we take Batozy's comments about her character into consideration. He said she's like a spoiled brat, always throwing a temper tantrum when she can't get what she wants. People like that often think the world revolves around them, and think they can get away with anything. She probably thought she was saving her sister from an unhappy marriage by killing the old man, and figured that if the police came after her, mommy and daddy would simply bail her out. Which," he added ruefully, "it looks like they will."

"Yeah, but they can't save her from a murder trial."

"Oh, you just wait and see. I'm sure they've already got some ace attorney lined up and stomping at the bit to find some legal loophole and get her off on a technicality. Mental anguish or psychological instability or some other legal mumbo jumbo. Mark my words, babe, that girl won't do a minute of jail time. Not even a second."

"She's in jail now."

"Not for long," Chase grunted, getting up. "Let's start dinner. I'm starving."

And so both our humans got up to start cooking, and

Dooley and I finally had a moment's respite from all this murder business to enjoy a nice and refreshing nap.

But of course that was before Gran barged in. "Hey, you guys," she said. "Wanna join us tonight on patrol?"

"I don't know, Gran," I said, now thoroughly sleepy. "We've been on patrol all day."

"Patrol? What patrol?"

"The murder? Though that seems to be solved now."

"Murder? What murder?"

"The murder of Rudyard van de Graaf," I said, and sincerely hoped I wouldn't have to give her a full report on the investigation.

"Oh, that," she said, with a throwaway gesture of her hand. "I'm talking about John Robie. We need to catch this guy before he burgles another home. And I gotta tell you that I've got a good feeling about this. I think tonight is the night that we'll catch the bastard."

"But we caught him already, Gran," said Dooley. "Chase and Odelia arrested him—or her—or them."

Gran stared at us, speechless for once. Though not for long. "And why didn't anyone bother to tell me?!"

"Because… you weren't there?" Dooley ventured.

"I don't care! I've got a phone. I've got email. Heck, I'm on WhatsApp!" She turned to Odelia and Chase. "Hey, you two!"

"Hey, Gran," said Odelia, oblivious of the woman's ire. "How was your day?"

"Why didn't you tell me that you caught John Robie?" she demanded heatedly.

"Oh, that's right. You haven't heard? We arrested Emma van de Graaf and her boyfriend. And it's all thanks to Max and Dooley."

Gran turned on her heel so fast she got dizzy for a moment, and seemed to totter. But she recovered fast. "You caught John Robie?"

"Well, Emma's cat Minnie revealed the whole thing," I explained. "She really gave the game away." I actually felt sorry for Emma. There was no way she could have foreseen this. Then again, stealing things is wrong, of course, even if you steal stuff that has already been stolen... by other thieves. Okay, so maybe there's a gray area there. Something to think about—or better yet, something for the judge to take into consideration.

"Minnie..." said Dooley dreamily. "I wonder what she's doing right now."

"Sleeping, probably," I said.

"Or thinking... of me."

"Focus, you two," said Gran. "I'm trying to find out where the whole thing broke down."

"What broke down, Gran?" I asked.

"This family's information structure! I'm the leader of the neighborhood watch, and as such I'm supposed to be in the know at all times. Only it looks to me as if I'm the last person to find out about this. So I demand answers, and I demand them right now!"

"Well, Minnie said..." I began.

"I don't care about Minnie or Mickey or whatever! Donald Duck himself might have told you—it doesn't matter! I want some cooperation here. Is that too much to ask?"

"Um..." I said, not really seeing what we could have done differently.

Gran turned around again. "From now on, you keep me in the loop, all right?"

"Sure, Gran," said Odelia. "What do you want to know?"

Gran stared at her for a moment, then her shoulders sagged. "You know what? I think I'm giving up on the watch."

Odelia looked up from her food prep. "You're not serious."

"I'm dead serious. I don't get cooperation from nobody.

Your uncle makes us a lot of promises I'm sure he won't keep. You won't keep me in the loop, and as for the cats—they seem to have forgotten I exist! No, I'm done with this nonsense. I'm done putting my life on the line for the safety and security of the ungrateful population of this stupid town."

Just then, Scarlett walked in. "Ready, hon?" she asked.

"We're going to a movie tonight," Gran snapped.

"A movie? I thought we were going patrolling?"

"No more patrolling. I'm done with the watch."

"What do you mean?"

"Done! No more watch! Hampton Cove can drown in crime for all I care. This is the end!" And with these words, she strode out, leaving Odelia and Chase to exchange a glance of significance and Scarlett to hurry after her partner in crime-fighting—or should I say former partner in crime-fighting?

But then sleep finally overtook me, and soon I was dead to the world.

CHAPTER 20

After enjoying a nice nap, it was time to go out and sing our hearts out at cat choir. And we weren't the only ones, since it seemed as if every night more and more cats gathered in the park to join up. I liked it. My friends liked it. And of course Shanille, the choir director, liked it. The only ones who were still reluctant to come on board and share the fun were the human neighbors. At some point one of them must have called the police, for I thought I saw the blue light of a cop car approach, the flickering light reflecting on the tree branches surrounding the playground that acts as our rehearsal space. But the cops must have understood that even cats have rights, and drove off again.

We might not be very good at what we do, but we all put our hearts and souls into our hobby, and I'm sure that after a while it will pay off. Maybe.

"So is it true that you caught John Robie?" asked Shanille.

"Yeah, we caught them," I said.

"Them?"

"Yeah, John Robie is actually a couple."

"A couple!"

"I don't believe it," said Harriet, looking annoyed by this development.

"What don't you believe, Harriet?" asked Shanille.

"VI Harriet for you," said Harriet. "I've changed my name."

Shanille arched a whisker, but didn't speak.

"Well, I don't think it's that simple," said Harriet, "that's all. And in fact I think this couple have nothing whatsoever to do with this whole John Robie business."

"We found the loot in their apartment," I pointed out.

"Planted there by the real John Robie."

"They confessed."

"To protect the real John Robie."

"They explained their motive for the break-ins."

"Oh, Max, you're so gullible," said Harriet with a sigh. "Of course they're going to give you some kind of explanation, but the truth is that you haven't caught him yet. But I have. Or at least I know where to find him."

"Oh? And where is that?"

"At the house, of course, where he'll murder again —tonight."

"John Robie will kill again?" asked Dooley. "Oh, no! But we have to stop him, Max!"

"We caught John Robie today, Dooley," I reminded him.

"Yes, but Harriet says it's not the real John Robie."

Oh, God.

"Look, if you want to help us stop him from murdering more people, you better join Brutus and me tonight," said Harriet. "Because not only do I know who the real John Robie is, I know when he's going to strike and why!"

"Okay, you got my attention," said Shanille. "Who is the real John Robie, Harriet?"

"VI Harriet. It stands for Very Important Harriet. All great detectives have VI before their names."

"No, they don't."

"And what would you know, Shanille?"

"VI Shanille to you, Harriet."

They both glowered at each other for a moment, then finally Harriet's desire to gloat won out over her desire to pick a fight with Shanille. "Okay, so I'll tell you who the real John Robie is. It's the butler!"

"Not again with the butler!" I cried. "The van de Graafs don't have a butler."

"That's because the butler is dead."

"The butler is dead!" Dooley cried. "Who killed him?" Then he thunked his head. "John Robie, of course! But why?"

"Oh, Dooley," said Harriet.

Brutus had now joined us. "What's going on?"

"I'm trying to explain who the real John Robie is," said Harriet. "But they keep interrupting me."

"She claims it's the butler," I told Brutus. "The dead butler."

"She's right," said Brutus. "After giving the matter considerable consideration, and working those little gray cells of ours to the bone, we've come to the only logical conclusion possible: the butler did it. Or at least the ghost of the butler."

"The ghost of the butler!" I cried, more incredulous by the second.

"Don't look at me like I've lost my mind, Max," said Harriet. "You'll see tonight that the butler is going to try to make more victims. And why, you ask? Because he's a socialist."

Shanille guffawed, I gawked and Dooley shrieked in terror. "A socialist butler!" my friend screamed. "Oh, no!"

"This is ridiculous," I said.

"Logical inference, Max," Harriet corrected my statement. "The van de Graafs are very rich, and they don't treat their staff the way they should be treated. For one thing, they don't pay them enough. So of course a certain resentment builds up over the years, and after a while that resentment turns into hatred and the desire to take revenge, and so they start looking for a ringleader to come up with a solution. And since everyone knows that a butler is the head of the household staff, they turn to him to lead the revolution."

"What revolution?!" I said, exasperated at having to listen to so much nonsense.

"Off with their heads, Max. It was the war cry of the French Revolution, and the same goes for the van de Graafs. The butler chose a simple yet efficient solution for their problems, and now he's carrying it out by picking off the people he works for one by one. Old man van de Graaf was his first victim, and I'm sure the rest of them will soon follow."

"We have to tell Odelia," said Dooley. "She has to stop the ghost of this socialist butler!"

"We're not telling Odelia a single thing," said Harriet. "She won't believe us."

"I don't believe you!" I said.

"Just you wait and see, Max. We're going over there tonight, and the moment you see all the dead bodies piling up, you'll have to admit that you were wrong to malign me."

"I'm not maligning you. I'm just telling you that you're dead wrong."

"Listen to yourself, Max. Dead. Wrong. Your subconscious knows that something is happening tonight. John Robie is on a killing spree, and we're the only ones who can stop him."

And here I thought I'd enjoy a nice relaxing evening!

CHAPTER 21

Seeing no other recourse than to prove Harriet wrong, I joined her and Brutus on their midnight excursion to the van de Graaf mansion. We arrived there in the dead of night, with not a single light illuminating the windows.

"See?" I said. "The house is asleep. No ghosts and especially no murderous ghosts."

"Oh, silly Max," said Harriet. "Ghosts don't need light. They can navigate perfectly fine without it. Come on, let's go."

"How are you going to get in?"

"Watch me," she said with a touch of mystery, and so we watched her, and followed her around the house.

"This is going to be good," said Brutus. "Just you wait and see."

"I'm waiting, and I'm seeing nothing," I told him.

"Oh, you're such a skeptic, Max. But for once in your life prepare yourself to be bested."

We approached what I knew was the kitchen, but instead of looking for a way in, Harriet turned away and headed into the backyard.

"Where are you going?" I asked.

"Trust me," she said.

I didn't trust her further than I could throw her, but what choice did I have but to follow in her paw-steps? Also, by this time my curiosity had been piqued. I know, I know, curiosity killed the cat. And I sincerely hoped it wouldn't kill me!

We reached a gazebo located a little further down the garden path, and headed inside. And suddenly, before our very eyes, Harriet... vanished!

"Hey, where did she go?" I asked.

"Neat trick, huh?" said Brutus. "We overheard Henrietta and Bru this afternoon. They said the secret passageways extend to this gazebo. Apparently when the van de Graafs built this place they made sure that they had a way out, in case they needed to escape."

"Now why would the van de Graafs need to escape?" I asked, as I studied the opening in the gazebo paneling more closely.

"People as rich as the van de Graafs are likely to create enemies, Max. And a hundred years ago those enemies came armed with pitchforks and torches. Now follow me."

And then he, too, disappeared into the dark opening.

"Max!" said Dooley. "I don't know if I can do this!"

"It's the same passageway we already explored, Dooley," I said. "There's nothing there except plenty of dead mice—and probably a lot of living ones."

"You go first," he said.

"What's taking you so long?" Brutus's irascible voice came. "Hurry up! We haven't got all night!"

Actually we did have all night, but I still heeded his words, and entered the hidden entrance, Dooley right on my heels.

And so once again we found ourselves in the secret passageway, only this time we descended deeper underground, where indeed a narrow corridor, dug out of the dark earth and kept from collapsing by plenty of sturdy wooden beams, led us in the direction of the main house. There was no electric light there, since Harriet or Brutus had yet to discover the switch, but what little light filtered in was enough to pick our way along.

And so soon the earthy smell gave way to a more musty one, and we knew we were on the right track.

"Now let's save some lives," said Brutus.

"Whose life do you want to save first?" I asked with a touch of sarcasm. But it was lost on the dapper duo.

"Royden and Abisha, of course," said Harriet. "The butler killed the patriarch of the family, now he'll go after the heir."

And so we moved up a rickety wooden staircase, and quickly were making our way to the second floor, where presumably Royden and Abisha had their bedroom.

"I just hope we don't bump into Henrietta and—aaargh!" Harriet cried.

"What are you doing here?" asked Henrietta, who'd suddenly emerged from the darkness like a… ghost. Behind her, Bru now also appeared.

"We're trying to save lives," Dooley explained.

"What are *you* doing here?" I asked.

"Oh, we like to move around this way," said Bru. "It's nice and comfy."

"And nobody sees us coming, which is even better," Henrietta explained.

"Harriet thinks that John Robie, who's the ghost of the socialist butler, is going to murder your entire family," said Dooley. "And so we are going to try and stop him."

Henrietta and Bru exchanged a glance, then burst out into hearty laughter.

"Good one!" said Henrietta, once she'd recovered from her bout of mirth.

"Yeah, great joke," said Bru.

"It's not a joke," said Harriet through gritted teeth. "That dead butler killed Rudyard, and now he's coming for Royden. Just you wait and see."

"But… we don't have a butler," said Henrietta.

"Yeah, Rudyard thought it was an unnecessary expense," Bru explained.

"It's a dead butler," Brutus said.

"A dead butler?" asked Bru. "I don't get it."

"It's a ghost butler," I said, my words eliciting another burst of gaiety from the duo.

"Let's go," said Harriet. "While we're wasting time with these two, John Robie is busy whetting his blade."

"Look, the dagger that was used to kill Rudyard was stolen by Emma, see?" I said, trying one last-ditch attempt to make Harriet and Brutus see the light. "So it can't have been some imaginary butler."

"So he made a copy. It's very easy nowadays to make a copy of anything, Max."

"Yeah, you can print it," said Brutus.

"Print it!"

"With a 3D printer. You can print anything with a 3D printer. Even a jumbo jet."

"Do try to keep up, Max," said Harriet.

And with these words, she trotted up the stairs, the leader of our small rescue team.

We finally arrived at the van de Graaf bedroom, and judging from the sounds of two people arguing, they hadn't run into Harriet's killer butler yet.

"I can't believe you'd still defend that man, Royden," Abisha was saying. "After everything he did."

"He was my dad. And whatever he did, he did for the good of the family."

"He called you a mealy-mouthed weasel! He said you had

the backbone of a jellyfish!"

"So? He might have expressed himself a little strongly from time to time, but—"

"He said that you marrying me was the biggest mistake you ever made!"

"It doesn't matter now, does it? He's dead."

"Yeah, and the cops think that Emma killed him."

"No one in their right mind could possibly think that Em is capable of murder."

"The police do. And they've got the evidence to back it up. Why, oh why didn't she tell us that she was the burglar?"

"Look, you and I both know for a fact that Em didn't kill Dad," said Royden. "So now all we have to do is make sure that the police know it, too."

"How? How, Royden?"

"I don't know," the man admitted.

We heard the creaking of bedsprings, a clear sign they were ready to turn in for the night.

"They're up very late," Dooley commented.

"They're always up late," Henrietta said. "The whole family suffers from insomnia."

"Do they ever use these passageways?" I asked.

"Oh, all the time. They love it. Rudyard himself used to sneak around here, especially when they had guests. He loved to spy on them, find out what they were up to."

"He was a strange man," said Bru.

"Strange, how?" I asked.

"Well, he seemed to harbor a strong hatred against his next of kin. In fact I don't think it's too much to say that he hated them all."

"Not all of them," said Henrietta. "He liked the girls."

"The girls?" I asked.

"Emma and Casey. He liked them best of all."

"He didn't like Royce?"

Bru made a face. "He hated Royce. Almost as much as he hated Royden."

"Odd," I said.

"He felt that Royden didn't live up to the expectations he had for his son and heir. In fact he considered skipping a generation and appointing one of the girls as his successor."

"What happened to Rudyard's wife?" asked Harriet.

"She died," said Henrietta. "Though I don't think he cared. The day she died, he went into the office—business as usual."

"How did she die?" I asked.

"In childbirth. Rudyard was unhappy that they only had the one son. He wanted more. More potential heirs to choose from. But his wife kept miscarrying. I think she must have suffered four of five miscarriages in a row. And the last one finally killed her."

"Rudyard was not a very nice man, was he?" asked Dooley.

"No, he certainly wasn't," Henrietta agreed. Then she frowned. "And now I think you better leave." It was as if she'd remembered that she wasn't supposed to be nice to us, or to answer our questions. We were, after all, intruders in her home.

"I swear to God, Royden," suddenly the voice of Abisha sounded through the wall loud and clear, "if Emma goes down for this murder, I'm holding you personally responsible."

"She won't go down for the murder. I've got the best lawyer lined up for her."

"For your sake I hope you're right. Cause if anything happens to that girl, you're a dead man!"

And I thought I could almost hear Royden's gulp through the wall!

CHAPTER 22

The next day, Dooley and I were happily napping in a corner of Odelia's office when the telephone rang.

"Chase?" we could hear Odelia say. She listened for a moment, then said, "I'll be outside," and hung up. She thought for a moment, then turned to us. "Emma and her boyfriend have been released on bail."

"So soon?" I asked.

"Yeah, looks like they've got a pretty savvy lawyer in their corner."

I'd told Odelia all about the conversations we overheard last night, and she had agreed that we needed to look a little deeper into Royden and Abisha. Emma had been caught red-handed, so to speak, but it wouldn't hurt to check out the rest of the family, too. Especially since they all seemed to have a solid motive to get rid of the old man. And it had to be said: Emma didn't strike either of us as the murderous type, no matter what Chase believed or what the evidence said.

Harriet and Brutus had decided to defy Henrietta and Bru, and had ended up spending the night at the van de

Graaf place, only arriving home early this morning. No one had been killed, though, so the killer butler theory had proved incorrect. Rather than admit defeat, Harriet had doubled down, and said that she was going out there again tonight, since she was the only one who could prevent another murder. And since they'd been up all night, they were now fast asleep at home.

"Let's go," said Odelia, grabbing her purse.

"Where are we going?" I asked.

"To talk to Royden and his wife again. And hopefully to some more people at the house."

And so five minutes later Chase picked us up in front of Odelia's office, and once again we were en route to the van de Graaf residence.

Royden and Abisha didn't seem particularly pleased to see us this time. No doubt the fact that Odelia and Chase had fingered their youngest daughter for murder had something to do with this.

"We talked to Guy Batozy yesterday," said Chase, not wasting time with preliminaries.

"Oh, that guy," said Abisha, rolling her eyes.

"And he said that there was no love lost between you and your father, Royden."

"Guy has no business spreading foul gossip..." Abisha began, but Royden placed a hand on her arm.

"It's all right," he said. "I don't think it's a big secret that my father and I weren't on the best of terms."

"But you still loved each other," Abisha tried valiantly to uphold appearances.

"No, we didn't," said her husband with a wan smile. "You see, my dad and I were never in sync, to use a modern phrase. He was what you might call a manly man—of a generation that believed in making your way through life by bullying people and running roughshod over anyone and anything that got in your way. I've always been more of the opinion that you have to treat people with kindness. My dad mistook that attitude for weakness, and never failed to berate me for what he felt was my ineptitude."

"Honey, you don't have to tell them all that."

"Yes, I do," Royden insisted. "You see, detective, I didn't like my dad, and he didn't like me, but underneath all that, I still loved him, and I like to think that he loved me—even though he found it very hard to express it."

"And what about the fact that he wanted to skip a generation and appoint one of your children his successor?" asked Chase.

Royden's jaw dropped. "How did you…"

"Is it true?"

Royden nodded. "He did threaten to leave everything to the kids, yes."

"Which one of your kids?"

Royden glanced to his wife, then bowed his head. "Casey," he said.

"Not Royce?"

"No, not Royce."

"Look, my father-in-law was a bastard, plain and simple," said Abisha. "Now I could give you some spiel about him belonging to a generation that wasn't used to men… liking other men, but that's bullshit. The plain truth is that he was a bitter, angry, vile old man, and I honestly think that the world is a better place without him."

"Abisha!" Royden cried.

"No, this needs to be said. But whatever we thought of him, or whatever he did to upset us, or to deliberately hurt us, we didn't kill him. Not Em, not me, not Royden—no one in this family would ever do such a thing."

"You can see how Emma's guilt looks very well-established at this point."

"That's for the judge to decide," said Abisha, a stern-faced look coming over her. "Now if there's nothing else…"

"One more thing," said Odelia, "if you don't mind. Your father-in-law had ordered a suit, to be made by Tallett. Did you know anything about that?"

"No, we didn't," said Abisha. "He had plenty of suits, so I don't see why he'd need another."

"He probably wanted to have a new suit for his birthday," said Royden. "My father loved a nice suit," he explained. "I guess he wanted to have one made as a surprise, and as a gift to himself."

"He was always doing stuff like that," said Abisha. "Secretive, that's just the way he was. He enjoyed sitting up there and concocting schemes, then spring them on us."

"He wasn't concocting schemes."

"Yes, he was. He was a schemer, and proud to be one."

"What I don't understand is why he'd use a cab?" said Odelia. "Why not use the car?"

"Dad hated waste," said Royden. "So he got rid of his chauffeur and his car. Said he could get around in a cab. Much cheaper and more efficient, too."

"He wanted Royden to get rid of his driver, too," said Abisha. "But Royden pointed out to him that with the number of times he used the car, he was actually much cheaper off with a chauffeured car than by taking cabs or Ubers. Dad didn't like it. He hated when he was being proved wrong."

"So he tried to get rid of your chauffeur?" asked Chase.

"Oh, yes, he did," said Royden. "In fact he actually fired him once. But I simply rehired him. Same with the butler. Though I ended up agreeing with him in the end. We really don't need a butler."

"But why did he try to cut corners like that?" asked Odelia. "Or was he having money problems?"

"No money problems," said Royden promptly. "Just being a penny pincher. Force of habit."

"Old people," said Abisha, but cut a quick look to Royden that spoke volumes.

So did the van de Graafs have money problems? It certainly looked that way.

Just then, a young man walked in. He looked the spitting image of his dad, only younger.

"What's going on?" asked the young man.

"This is Royce," said Royden, introducing his son. "Royce, these people are from the police. They're investigating your grandpa's murder."

"Oh," said Royce, stiffening. "So you're the ones who arrested my sister? Nice one."

"May we have a word, sir?" asked Chase, not deterred by the young man's words.

"If you must," said Royce.

"Just get it over with," Abisha advised. "Sooner or later you're going to have to talk to them anyway."

"He looks very much like his dad," said Dooley.

"The spitting image," I agreed.

"Just like Emma and Casey look like their mom."

"Indeed."

"So why is it that human children often look like their parents, Max?"

"I thought you could tell me, Dooley. You're the one who watches the Discovery Channel all the time."

"I think I must have missed that documentary."

"It's got something to do with DNA," I said.

He gave me a puzzled look. "I don't see what the NBA has got to do with anything."

"Not the NBA. DNA. Genes, Dooley. It's all about the genes."

But luckily before I was forced to launch into an explanation on the double helix and all of that stuff, Royden and Abisha left the room, and then it was time to ask a couple of tough questions to Royce van de Graaf.

CHAPTER 23

"Look, Em is just about the sweetest girl on the planet," Royce began, "so if you think she could possibly do the old man harm, think again."

"The evidence against her is pretty convincing, Royce," Chase pointed out.

"I don't care about any evidence. I'm telling you that I know my sister, and she would never do this—so you better start over, cause you're obviously mistaken."

"Let's talk about you for a moment, shall we?" Chase suggested. "First off, where were you yesterday afternoon between three and four?"

"I was on my way over here, actually. I wanted to talk to Grandad. Only I changed my mind and turned back."

"You were alone in the car?"

"I was," said the young man with a touch of defiance. He continued to be very prickly, and was clearly not happy about being interviewed.

"So no one can confirm that you were in your car, driving here and then back home?"

"No one," he said curtly.

"Where do you live, Royce?" asked Odelia.

"In town. Not far from where Em lives, actually, and Casey. Even though we all flew the nest, somehow we ended up living close to each other."

"How would you describe your relationship with your grandad, Royce?" asked Chase.

He shrugged and studied his fingernails for a moment. "I was fond of the old guy, and I like to think that he was fond of me."

"A normal grandfather-grandson relationship in other words?"

"Absolutely."

"Your mom and dad told us that Rudyard wasn't happy about you being married to a man, though. And we heard that he even refused to come to the wedding. Said you weren't his grandson anymore. He even threatened to cut you from his will. That doesn't sound like the kind of relationship most people have with their grandfather."

"Look, if you already know all this, why ask me?"

"Because I want to hear it from you, Royce."

"Okay, so maybe my grandad wasn't such a swell guy. And maybe he had some old-fashioned ideas about men and women and marriage and all of that. But that doesn't mean I hated him and wanted to kill him, if that's what you're working up to."

"What did you want to talk to him about?" asked Odelia.

"Oh, just this and that. Family stuff, you know."

"No, we don't know, Royce," said Chase. "So why don't you tell us?"

Royce uttered a deep sigh, and looked as if he was utterly bored with this conversation. "Maybe I should get a lawyer. If you're going to go all good cop, bad cop on me and all."

"We're just trying to find out what happened to your grandfather," said Odelia.

"I thought you had it all figured out already? Em did it. Because the old man had some Nazi knife in his collection or something. Craziest thing I ever heard."

Now that he put it like that, it did sound a little iffy, I thought. Then again, Emma did seem very serious about her mission to return this stolen art to its rightful owners.

"All we're doing here is following the evidence, Royce," Odelia said, leaning in and holding out her hands. "And the evidence right now is pointing to your sister. But we're keeping an open mind—of course we are. And so we're looking at every possibility. But your sister did admit that she stole that dagger. And the dagger does have her fingerprints on it, and only her fingerprints. And since it is the murder weapon, we had to take her into custody. Plus, she burgled the homes of at least three other families. So she may be the sweetest girl in the world, just as you say, but she's also the cat burglar we've been looking for."

"Okay, so she is John Robie, but that doesn't mean she killed my grandad." But he was frowning now, and thinking about Odelia's words. "You're saying her fingerprints were on the dagger?"

"They were, Royce, so you can see how that looks."

"Yeah, I don't know how that happened," he murmured. He rubbed his temple with the palm of his hand. "Look, I just wanted to see Grandad to tell him I was coming to his birthday party, and I was bringing Jeff."

"Jeff?"

"My husband. So whether he liked it or not, we were coming. But then as I was driving over here I figured why bother, you know? Why pick a fight with the old man?"

"What does he do for a living, your husband?" asked Chase, always a stickler for the correct routine.

"Um, he's a designer. Designs menswear. He's got a

boutique here in town, and another one in Manhattan, though he's got his atelier in Hampton Cove."

"And what do you do, Royce?" asked Odelia.

Royce grinned. "Can't you tell? I'm a model. That's how me and Jeff met. I was doing one of his shows, and he thought I looked so good in his designs that he hired me for a shoot. One thing led to another, and three years later we got married."

"Without your grandpa present."

Royce grimaced. "Yeah, I still can't believe he pulled a stunt like that. He told me he wouldn't show up, and I didn't believe him. But of course I should have known he was serious."

"Did you ever patch things up with him?"

"Not really. I tried to talk to him. Even brought Jeff along one night so he could get to know him, and see what a great guy he is. But nothing doing. He kicked us both out." He grinned. "Talk about a ballbuster. In some ways you gotta admire the guy. To be so politically incorrect all the time, and not to give a damn about what anyone thought about him—that takes guts. Or a lousy personality. Though I have to say that when I was a kid we got along great, me and Grandad. In fact for a while he said he was going to leave me the whole kit and caboodle one day, figuring Dad was too lame to handle the pressure of running a multimillion-dollar business. But then as I got older I guess he soured on me."

"So who was going to take over the business if not your dad or you?" asked Odelia.

"Casey, of course. She was the chosen one. Though to be absolutely honest it's going to be tough going for Case."

"And why is that?"

"Because we're dead broke, that's why."

"What do you mean?"

He shrugged. "Didn't my dad tell you? My grandfather

was so persistent lately about Casey marrying Zalman not because of some romantic notion about the two families coming together, but because it was the only way to save the family holding from collapsing into a heap of insolvency." He gestured around himself. "This place? Mortgaged to the hilt, just like every other property the family owns. No, Casey refusing to marry Zalman is probably going to kill us off for good. It will be the end of the van de Graafs. We had a good run for oh, about a century? But then we blew it."

CHAPTER 24

Cyprian Mulhearn had agreed to see us at his club. His golf club, that is. He'd even suggested Chase and Odelia play a round of golf with him, but since neither were proficient in the game, they'd respectfully declined.

So now we sat on the terrace of the Riviera Country Club being served with drinks—the human contingent with proper drinks, Dooley and me with a dish of water—and watching what is commonly termed the first hole, where two players were teeing up, as the vernacular goes, and taking aim at a little white ball poised on top of a little stick.

"It's a funny game, isn't it, Max?" said Dooley, as we watched one of the men, dressed in white, make a few practice swings and then finally hit the ball and watch it fly.

"It is," I agreed. "Grown men hitting a ball with a stick. I wonder what's so enjoyable about that."

"I think it's because when they do it right, the ball ends up in a hole," said Dooley.

"So? I don't see the point."

"It's a sexual thing, Max," said Dooley, causing me to regard him with surprise.

"What do you mean?"

"Haven't you noticed how most of these ball sports are played by men? And it's always the same thing: how to get a ball into a hole. I saw a documentary on the Discovery Channel the other night, and a professor in psychology explained it's all about sublimation."

"Sublimation, huh?" I said, having a hard time suppressing a smile.

"I didn't understand it at the time, but I've been thinking, and he was right. Men are always hitting on women, hoping to score. And ball sports are a sublimation of that."

I regarded my friend with marked interest. "I think you watch too much Discovery Channel, Dooley," I said.

"Oh, no, it's very interesting, Max. You can really learn a lot."

"I'll bet you can."

The man who'd hit the ball was now making a sort of yipping sound. Clearly his ball had hit the target, and he'd come this much closer to winning against his opponent.

"Bad business," Mr. Mulhearn was saying. "I talked to Rudyard only last week. He was really looking forward to this wedding, and frankly so was I."

"So the wedding was going ahead?" asked Chase.

"Oh, absolutely. Rudyard wouldn't have it any other way, and of course I was glad for this opportunity for our two families to finally come together."

The man looked to be about Rudyard's age, and was dressed in a white golf shirt, white slacks and white golf shoes. He actually looked very fit and healthy for his age, and it made me wonder if there was more to golf than even Dooley had fathomed. I'd never looked upon the game as anything more than a silly pastime for the idle rich, but maybe there was a fitness aspect about it after all.

"As we understood, both Casey and Zalman were

opposed to the wedding," said Odelia. "They're both in love with other people, but felt trapped by this arrangement between yourself and Rudyard."

The old man sighed deeply. "I know. Zalman told me as much. And if I'm absolutely honest I was hoping that they'd change their mind at some point. Did you know that arranged marriages are less likely to end up in divorce than the other kind? So there is something to be said for two people being thrown together." When he caught Odelia's frown, he added, "Though of course if they really didn't want to marry, I wasn't going to make them."

"Rudyard was. He even threatened to leave his entire fortune to his favorite charities if the wedding didn't go through."

"I thought that was taking things too far."

"Did you talk to him about this?"

"Of course. But he was adamant."

"Isn't it true, Mr. Mulhearn," said Chase, "that there was another aspect to the matter?"

"What aspect?"

"A reliable source has told us that Rudyard was facing financial difficulties, and a marriage with a Mulhearn would go a long way toward, shall we say, making those go away?"

Cyprian Mulhearn's face twisted into an amused smile. "Who told you that?" But when Chase merely stared at him, he finally relented. "Well, it's true, of course. But that wasn't Rudyard's fault. It's that son of his who made a couple of very unwise investments in the last couple of years, causing the family fortune to take a serious hit. So an influx of cash would have made all the difference."

"That bad, is it?"

Cyprian nodded. "Pretty much. I don't know the full picture, of course, but as Rudyard gave me to understand, the van de Graaf holding is taking on water and sinking fast."

"And you're saying that Rudyard blamed his son?"

"Yes, he did. He spoke about Royden in terms I won't repeat here, but let's just say he didn't have much confidence in the man. In fact the last time we spoke he was considering removing his son from his role and putting Casey in charge."

"Casey? Why not Royce?"

"Because he said Royce took too much after his dad, while Casey was more like Rudyard himself: she had a good head on her shoulders, unlike Royden and Royce."

Odelia and Chase exchanged a look, and so did Dooley and myself.

"Look, business acumen sometimes skips a generation," said Cyprian. "And sometimes the next generation is flawed and all you can do is try and save the company from their ineptness. It was Rudyard's big disappointment that neither his son or his grandson had what it took. Casey has talent, though. In spades. But if Rudyard put her in charge, it would mess up the relationship with her dad and brother. Also, without an influx of fresh capital there isn't a lot she can salvage. So Rudyard had some tough decisions to make."

"Couldn't he have gone to the banks?" asked Chase.

"Banks were reluctant to throw good money after bad."

"Third-party investors?"

"They'd want control, and Rudyard wasn't prepared to allow control to be wrested away from the family. No, the only way to save the company was that marriage." He took a sip from his pink-colored drink. "And now that it looks as if the wedding is off..." He gave us a meaningful look.

"You're not prepared to save them, Mr. Mulhearn?" asked Odelia.

He smiled. "I'm a businessman, Mrs. Kingsley. If my grandson had married Casey van de Graaf, that would have been a different matter. But now? Now it's just business. And right now, an investment in the van de Graafs is bad business—pure and simple."

"And with your friend gone…"

Cyprian's smile faltered as he glanced across the green. "He was a good friend, and I am really sad that he's gone." He turned to Chase. "Catch the bastard, will you?" There was a sudden vehemence in his voice. And it was clear that he might be a hardened businessman, but in Rudyard he'd lost a good friend and confidant.

"We will," Chase promised. "You have my word."

CHAPTER 25

We'd just reached the car when Chase got a phone call from the Chief. He listened for a moment, then cursed inwardly. "Where do you want us to go first, Chief? The hospital? Will do." He disconnected and answered Odelia's quizzical look by saying curtly, "Vincent Rebela has been involved in a hit-and-run accident. He's in the hospital. And there's been a murder. Looks like a burglary-related homicide."

"Let's go," said Odelia, and we all piled into the car and moments later Chase was stomping his foot down on the accelerator and his tires kicked up gravel, spraying a couple of Teslas and Porsches with debris. A golfer, who'd been busy placing his bag of golf clubs in the back of his Porsche Coupé, swung his fist in anger.

"How did it happen?" asked Odelia.

"He was out for a run when he was scooped up by a passing car. They didn't stop to see if he was all right, but left him on the road for dead. A witness called 911."

"Is he badly injured?"

"The Chief didn't know."

"Do you think it's connected with the John Robie business?"

"I don't know, babe. I'm as much in the dark here as you are."

"You want to know what I think, Max?" asked Dooley.

"Mh?" I said. I'd been thinking about this hit-and-run business, and wondering, like Odelia, if it was connected to the events of the last couple of days.

"I think that people who are happy and secure in their relationship don't go in for golf."

"Oh, Dooley," I said with a sigh.

"No, hear me out, Max. If a man has no issues getting together with a woman, there's absolutely no reason for him to go chasing a little white ball and try to land it in a hole, is there? It's only the frustrated ones, the ones who get rejected all the time, and who can't get a date, who turn to golf."

"I'm sure the golf enthusiasts will be thrilled to hear that, Dooley."

"It's all about psychology, Max. And psychology doesn't lie."

"I'm sure you're right," I said.

We'd arrived at the hospital, and it didn't take Chase more than a few minutes to find out where Vincent had been taken. He was out of surgery, but was still in intensive care, and as we entered his room, we found Emma sitting next to a heavily bandaged man.

"Who's the mummy, Max?" asked Dooley.

"I think that's Vincent," I said.

"How can you be sure? He's completely covered in bandages."

"Emma's holding his hand. She wouldn't be holding the hand of a stranger, now would she?"

Dooley laughed. "It would be very awkward if they

removed those bandages and it turns out she'd been sitting next to the bed of a complete stranger, wouldn't it, Max?"

"Yes, Dooley. That would be hysterical."

"What happened?" asked Odelia, as she drew up a chair.

Emma shook her head. She'd clearly been crying, as her eyes were red and she was as pale as the sheet covering her boyfriend. "He was out for a jog, to clear his head, and some car came out of nowhere and hit him, then drove right off."

"Any idea who the driver was?" asked Chase. He'd taken out his notebook.

"There was a witness. An older lady walking her dog. She said it was an SUV. Black or dark blue, she wasn't sure. She didn't get a good look at the driver."

"Did she get the license plate?"

"I don't know," said Emma. "I'd just gone shopping, and I happened to drive past when I suddenly recognized Vince's…" Her voice faltered for a moment, and Odelia pressed her hand in hers. "Vince always wears this orange high-vis vest when he goes jogging. I saw it, and immediately I knew—just knew. So I parked and ran over, and it was him."

"You talk to the witness?" asked Chase.

"Just briefly. The ambulance—they worked on him for a while, and then took him here. I followed them—he was in surgery for the past hour and a half."

"Will he be all right?" asked Odelia.

She shook her head. "I don't know. They're not telling me anything!"

Odelia hugged the distraught young woman, and Chase frowned darkly at the patient, as if blaming him for what had happened. I could understand the cop's frustration. It's hard to solve a murder when one of the prime suspects might not survive a traffic accident.

"Oh, and there's this," said Emma, and took something

out of her pocket. "I was going to bring this to the police station." She held out a small circular object, connected with a couple of wires.

"What's that?" asked Odelia.

"I found this in the kitchen. I pulled the shades and this fell out."

Chase took a small plastic baggie from his pocket and bagged the item, then studied it closely. "Looks like a listening device," he finally determined. "A bug."

Emma frowned. "A bug?"

Chase nodded. "Looks like someone bugged your apartment."

"Oh, God," said Emma. "What is happening!"

But before they could thresh the thing out further, a doctor, accompanied by a nurse, entered the room, and asked for everyone, except Emma, to leave.

And so we all left the room, and took up position in the corridor.

Chase took the bug out of his pocket and stared at it some more, as if hoping it would tell him something about who had placed it in Emma and Vincent's apartment. Of course the bug stayed mum, as bugs do, except when connected to a machine of some kind.

"Didn't you say there had been a murder?" asked Odelia, bringing her husband back to earth.

"Oh, right!" said Chase, jumping up. "Totally forgot about that. Let's go."

And we were off again. It's odd. Sometimes nothing happens for weeks on end, and then suddenly it's just one thing after another. That's the life of a cat sleuth, I guess.

CHAPTER 26

Once again we were in the car, with Chase driving us at a great rate of speed—and flashing lights—in the direction of yet another crime scene.

"We have to talk to this witness," said Odelia. "The one who saw Vincent get scooped up."

"I know," said Chase.

"Poor Emma."

"She's still our number-one suspect, babe."

"I know, but still. She must be feeling persecuted by now. Do you think she actually found that bug, or is she just trying to convince us that there was a break-in, and that someone stole that dagger from her?"

"As I said before, it all sounds pretty fishy to me. That whole break-in business is probably just a smokescreen."

"It does look very bleak for her, doesn't it?" She settled down in her seat, prepared to go over the whole case again. "But if she didn't do it, then who did? It must have been someone who knew that she was John Robie and that she took that dagger."

"So a friend? Or a family member?"

"She says she didn't confide in anyone. That apart from Vincent no one knew that she was the cat burglar."

"Unless of course her story is true, and someone did bug her apartment, and found out that way."

"But who would bug Emma and Vincent's place?"

"Emma's dad? Trying to keep tabs on his daughter? The man might look like a pussy cat but when you're running a multimillion-dollar company you're bound to have something of a shark in you, as well."

"Royden did hate his dad, and vice versa. But his alibi is solid. The helicopter pilot confirms that he was in the air at the time Rudyard was killed. Besides, no dad would try and put the blame on his own daughter. And then there's Abisha. Rudyard's constant put-downs must have really annoyed the hell out of her. So maybe she'd finally had enough, especially now that he was pressuring her daughter into a marriage that she didn't want."

"Could be," Chase allowed. "But would she save one daughter by throwing another daughter under the bus? Sounds unlikely."

"Or how about Royce? He was effectively being sidelined by Rudyard, just because he was gay."

"Don't forget what Cyprian told us: Rudyard thought that both Royden and Royce were incompetent, and wanted Casey to run the company."

"And that leaves Casey, who had a big motive for doing away with her grandfather."

"But why would Casey incriminate her own sister?" asked Chase. "Those two seem to be so close."

"Yeah, that doesn't make any sense."

We'd arrived at our destination, and Chase parked his car right next to another police vehicle.

The house where the burglary-slash-murder had taken place was a modest row house that had seen better days. The paint on the facade was peeling in places, and so was the paint on the windows and the front door. A geranium plant had been placed on the windowsill but its owner had unfortunately been very stingy with water, and the plant was hanging on by a thread.

The door of the premises was open, and a cop was guarding the entrance, allowing Chase and Odelia passage with a kindly greeting. He glanced down at Dooley and me and gave us a grin. Every cop in Uncle Alec's police force knew that Odelia rarely traveled alone.

"So what do we have here?" asked Chase once we'd entered the living room. The body of a well-fed man lay face down in the center of the room, half on the carpet and half on the stone floor.

Abe Cornwall got up out of a crouch, his knees creaking in protest, and announced, "He's dead, all right."

"I thought as much," said Chase with an amused little grin. "But how did he get that way, that's what I would like to know, Abe."

"Knock on the head with a blunt object would do the trick," said Abe as he removed his plastic gloves. "And most likely the object in question is lying right there." He pointed to a bust of a man whose hair looked a lot like Abe's: frizzy and voluminous.

"Beethoven?" asked Odelia.

"Oh, is that who it is?" said Chase as he studied the bust, which was lying on its side on the floor next to the dead man.

It was a plaster bust, and looked pretty heavy.

"You can do some serious damage with this thing," Chase concluded.

"Traces of blood and hair on the bust," said Abe curtly. "Traces of plaster in the head wound. I'll have to check, but it looks pretty conclusive to me."

"One single blow?" asked Chase.

"No, several," said Abe. "Probably three or four. I'll be able to tell you more after I've had him on my slab."

Odelia gulped a little, and her face turned green. Chase, though, was unaffected. When you've been an NYPD detective long enough, as he had been in a previous life, probably you got hardened against these aspects of a murder inquiry.

It was clear that the place had been thoroughly ransacked: drawers had been opened and their contents deposited on the floor, shelves cleared of the trinkets they'd held, and the place looked as if a small tornado had hit it with gale force.

"Looks like burglary, all right," Chase concluded. "Burglar probably thought he was alone in the house, but then the owner or tenant walked in on him, a struggle ensued and so the burglar hit him over the head."

"It must be great when you can solve a murder in five seconds," said Abe with a touch of sarcasm. "Well, I'm out of here," he said, then gestured to one of his people. "You can take him now," and walked out.

A uniformed officer stepped into the room, wrinkled her nose when she caught sight of the victim, then approached Chase. "I talked to the neighbors, sir," she said.

"And? Did you get an ID on the victim?"

"Yes, sir. A Justin Troller. Actor."

"An actor, huh?"

"Yes, sir. One of the neighbors is also the landlord. Says that Troller was an exemplary tenant. Always paid his rent on time, kept the house neat and clean—no complaints. One of the other neighbors says that Mr. Troller was a friendly man, always said hello. Didn't have a bad word to say about him. He used to be an actor on the stage in New York, but hadn't had much luck, so he moved back here a couple of years ago, and now did most of his work for an agency in town."

"What kind of work?"

"As a clown, sir, at children's birthday parties."

"A clown?"

There was indeed a portrait of a clown, which presumably had been hanging on the wall, but was now on the floor.

Odelia picked it up and she and Chase studied it for a moment.

"Poor man," said Odelia with feeling. "Why break in here? Doesn't look like there was a lot to steal."

"Could be a drug addict," said Chase. "They get desperate and will do anything for their next fix." He gestured to the wall, where a flatscreen television had been affixed, but where now only ripped-out cables could be seen. The stereo, too, had been taken from the cabinet underneath the TV.

Just then, Chase's phone chimed again, and he picked up with a curt, "Chief?" He listened for a moment, then cursed under his breath. "Okay, we'll be there in five." He disconnected and said, with a look of exasperation on his face, "Altercation at the van de Graafs. We better get there quick, before there's another murder in the family."

CHAPTER 27

"It's a busy day today, isn't it, Max?" said Dooley as once more we were being chauffeured to the van de Graaf mansion. "Lots of crimes being committed by lots of people."

"Yeah, it is one of those days," I confirmed.

"If only these people would take up golf," said my friend, "the world would be a safer place."

"How do you figure that?"

"Well, it's obvious that all these criminals are frustrated men, and frustrated men can either turn to golf, or turn to crime. Unfortunately a lot of them turn to crime."

"It's a theory," I admitted with a smile.

"I think we should talk to Uncle Alec, Max."

"What for?"

"He and Charlene should actively encourage men to take up golf. It would make this town a much safer place. And if ex-criminals would be encouraged to go golfing, they might not return to their old criminal life."

"I very much doubt whether golf will keep criminals from recidivism, Dooley."

"Reci-what, Max?"

"Recidivism. Taking up their criminal habits after they've been released from prison."

"Well, and I think that golf is the best thing against rectificism."

"You could be right," I said. After all, as far as I knew, Dooley's novel theory had never been tested. And if the Discovery Channel's psychologists said it was so...

Chase parked in front of the big house, and he and Odelia hurried out. I have to admit Dooley and I followed with some reluctance. I still remembered being lured and locked up in the passageways by Henrietta and Bru, and even though the duo seemed to have warmed to us to a certain degree, I was still wary.

We arrived just in time to catch the tail end of what looked like one of those family dust-ups that are all the rage when a family member has died and the will is being read.

The lawyer whose assistance we had so appreciated was there, and so were all the van de Graafs—except Emma, for obvious reasons.

Royce seemed to be the one with a major chip on his shoulder, for when we entered the study, he was pointing an accusatory finger at his sister Casey, and his face was red.

"You did this," he said. "You and the old man conspired against me!"

"Don't be ridiculous," said Casey, who stood with her arms folded across her chest. "I had no idea what was in Grandad's will."

"No one knew, Royce," said Royden, trying to calm down his son.

"Oh, I'll bet you knew all about it," said Royce. "In fact I'll bet you were all in on it together, weren't you!"

"What's going on?" asked Chase as he stepped to the fore, and bodily inserted himself between the verbally sparring parties.

"Mr. Conlan just read the will," said Abisha, "and it contained a few surprises, to say the least."

"He cut me out!" Royce cried, the veins in his neck standing out like cords. "Looks like I've got no place in this family anymore!"

A well-dressed man of about the same age as Royce now stepped forward. "Honey, don't get upset," he said.

"No, Jeff!" said Royce, swiping his husband's proffered hand away. "They've been wanting to get rid of me for years —and now they've finally succeeded!"

"That's not true, son," said Royden. "Nobody is trying to get rid of anybody."

"So how do you explain the will, then? Huh, Dad?"

They all stared at the lawyer, who merely shrugged and took off his glasses. He was just doing his job, his facial expression seemed to say, and he was right, of course. He was just the messenger, and judging from the way he gathered up his things and made haste to depart from the scene, he very much wanted to avoid being tarred and feathered.

"The will of my late grandfather," said Casey, "stipulates that I inherit everything."

"I'm the oldest son!" Royce screamed, thumping his chest. "I'm the heir!"

"Oh, will you shut up?" said Abisha, who clearly had had it with her son's antics.

"This isn't fair," said Royce, shaking his head. "He can't do this. He just can't."

"We'll make some kind of arrangement," said Royden. "Don't you worry, son. We'll fix this."

Casey gave her father a curious look. Clearly she was wondering if her dad proposed to ignore Rudyard's last will and testament.

"Oh, just leave it," Royce snapped, slapping his dad's arm away, and walked off on a huff. His husband dawdled for a moment, then followed his partner. A door slammed, and peace finally returned.

"What a mess," said Royden, dragging a hand through his hair.

"Odd that the lawyer didn't tell us about this," Chase said to Odelia in an undertone.

"I already found it very strange that he told us what was in the will in the first place," she returned.

"Not so strange," said Abisha, who had very sharp ears, apparently. "This is a new will. One we discovered in Rudyard's study this morning. Even Conlan had no idea he made it."

"Is it valid?" asked Chase.

"Oh, I'll bet it is. It was witnessed by the cook and the gardener, and according to Conlan it is absolutely valid. He was as surprised as we all are, apparently."

"The original appointed me the successor," said Royden, who looked a little flustered. "But apparently my dad wasn't… happy with my work lately, so he decided to carry out a threat he sometimes made. He skipped a generation and selected Casey as his successor."

"I honestly had no idea," Casey reiterated her earlier statement.

"I know, honey," said her mother. "And it's fine. We'll work it out."

"So you're in charge of the holding now?" asked Odelia.

Casey nodded. "Looks like."

"Well, at least the old man didn't give the whole kit and caboodle to charity," said Abisha. "And now if you'll excuse me, I want to go and pay a visit to Vincent."

"Yeah, me, too," said Casey. "How is he?" She directed this question to Odelia.

"I'm not sure," said Odelia. "The doctor kicked us out of the room."

Casey smiled. "Annoying habit of doctors. Let's, go, Mom. Dad? Are you coming?"

"Yes. Yes, of course," said Royden, who stood plunged in thought. If you've just discovered that you've been sidelined by your own dad, it provides food for thought.

We walked along with Casey to her sporty Mini Cooper. "Do you think your brother will be all right?" asked Odelia.

"Oh, sure. Royce makes a lot of noise, but he's always been more bark than bite."

"It's odd. When we talked to him he seemed to be relaxed about his position on the sidelines. I'm surprised that he's so upset now."

"I think he was expecting the death of Grandad to change all that. That it would finally allow him to take up the role of son and heir. Vindication after all those years of humiliation. And now Grandad has dealt him this final blow from across the grave and he's furious. Especially since Royce could use the money."

"He's in financial trouble?"

"Royce has been pouring money into Jeff's design business for years. To the tune of millions if the rumors are correct."

"I thought Jeff was a successful designer?"

"That's what he'd like people to think. The truth is that without Royce's money, he would have gone belly-up years ago. Royce is keeping him afloat, and hemorrhaging money as a consequence."

"Now that you're in charge, are you going to put a stop to that?"

Casey shrugged. "Honestly? I have no idea. This is very unexpected for me, too, you know. I'll have to think about it. And now if you'll excuse me, Em needs me."

She got into her car, and moments later was racing off, followed by a second car, carrying her mom and dad.

"I guess this is our cue, babe," said Chase, and soon we were mobile, too.

"So Royce was having money trouble," said Chase. "Looks like a great motive for murder to me, especially if he was expecting to receive a windfall when Rudyard died."

"Yes, and judging from his anger, this new will was the last thing he expected."

"If Royce is the killer, or his husband—or both—their murderous plans didn't pay off."

"I really can't believe Royce would break into his sister's apartment to steal that dagger and put her in the frame, though."

"Not Royce, maybe, but what about the husband? If his business really is losing money hand over fist, he could have decided to get rid of the old man."

"We better look into Casey's claims," said Odelia. "Find out what the financial situation really looks like for Mr. Jeff Malkan."

"In the meantime, why don't we pay a little visit to our unsuccessful star designer?"

CHAPTER 28

We found Mr. Malkan in his atelier, busily putting the final touches on his next collection. A male model stood in the center of the spacious room, dressed in something that looked like a collection of rags adorned with sprigs of holly. Which is how I knew we were in the presence of genius, since all geniuses are slightly—or a lot—eccentric.

"What is that man wearing, Max?" asked Dooley.

"I'm not sure, but it's probably brilliant," I said, "and very expensive."

"He looks like a scarecrow."

"Probably the theme of the winter collection." Or is it the fall collection? Or of course it could have been the spring collection. Since I have yet to patronize New York Fashion Week, I have to admit I'm a rube when it comes to high fashion.

"Mr. Malkan!" Chase called out as we walked up to the designer.

The man glanced up, then when he saw Chase actually affected a smile. "Detective Kingsley. I didn't expect to see you again so soon."

"This isn't a social call, I'm afraid," said Chase. "We wanted to ask you where you were when your husband's grandfather was killed."

"Remind me, when was this again?"

"Yesterday afternoon, between three-thirty and four o'clock."

"Between three-thirty and four… well, I was right here, slaving away on my collection. You can ask Fabio—he'll tell you."

Fabio, who was an effeminate young man, gave us a supercilious look and nodded. "We were here, sir. Working hard."

"And what about your husband? Was he also here?" asked Chase.

"Oh, no. Royce was out… doing whatever it is he does. We don't live in each other's pockets, detective. A relationship needs space to breathe. And I like to give Royce that space."

"He claims that he was on his way to see his grandfather but changed his mind."

The designer held up his hands. "Well, there you are."

"Isn't it true that your company is hemorrhaging money, and that you needed that inheritance from your husband's grandfather?"

Jeff cut a quick glance to Fabio, then decided that these financial matters didn't concern him, and said curtly, "Follow me, please."

So we followed him to an office located in the corner of his atelier.

He took a seat behind a large desk, cluttered with designs and fabric samples and gave Chase a pointed look. "Please don't discuss my financial affairs in front of my models. Especially Fabio. He'll tell the others, and before you know it, they'll think I'm on the verge of going bust and they'll run for the hills and I won't have a model left for my show."

"But isn't it true that you are facing financial difficulties?" Chase insisted.

"We may have a slight cash flow problem right now," said the designer, studiously studying a fingernail, "but as anyone will tell you that is all part of running a business. The ebb and flow of capital is something you learn to deal with—and we *were* dealing with it," he said emphatically.

"Isn't it also true that Royce is keeping your business afloat? And that without his financial support you would be finished?"

The look he now gave Chase was positively icy, and when he spoke again, there was an acerbity to his tone that would have served him well in an episode of Project Runway. "I can promise you that those are all lies, detective. Who told you that?"

"We have our sources," said Chase lightly.

"Well, it's not true. My business is financially sound, and while it is true that Royce supplied the startup capital, I've been self-supporting ever since. In fact I've been turning a very healthy profit for the past five years. And so what if I keep reinvesting my profits into the business? That's a well-established practice and the only way to keep expanding." He waved an annoyed hand. "And now if you could please go. You're hampering my creative process with these baseless insinuations of yours."

Chase planted both hands on the desk and leaned in. "You know what else isn't good for the creative process? Murder. So I hope you're telling me the truth, Jeff. Cause if you aren't, I'm going to find out."

Jeff gulped a little, then said, "I would never lie to the police, Detective Kingsley. My parents didn't raise me like that."

. . .

"He looked very unhappy, didn't he, Max?" said Dooley once we'd left the designer to go about his business. "I don't think he liked the way Chase kept asking him all kinds of questions."

"He's got a pretty good motive for murder," I said, "and so does his husband."

"But they're not getting any money, are they?"

"No, but they didn't know that. As far as they were concerned the death of Rudyard was going to open up a whole new world of wealth for them. Only Rudyard surprised them all."

One block down from where Jeff Malkan worked on his new collection, Creative Enterprises was located, the company Justin Troller worked for. And since Chase and Odelia were trying to solve several murders at once, they decided to drop in and find out what Mr. Troller had been up to lately.

The man who owned Creative Enterprises was a round-faced individual with a thin strip of beard that seemed to run all around his face. In the middle it was crossed by a mustache that ran from ear to ear. The end result was disconcerting, to say the least.

"Mr. Claude Joki?" asked Odelia once we'd set foot in the man's small office. "Hi, my name is Odelia Poole and I'm a civilian consultant assisting the police. And this is Chase Kingsley, detective in charge of the murder of one of your employees—Justin Troller."

"Oh, of course, Justin. I heard about it," said Mr. Joki as he got up from behind his desk and shook hands with Odelia and Chase. "Terrible business. What happened, exactly?"

"We think he caught a burglar and was killed as a consequence," said Chase.

"What can you tell us about Justin?" asked Odelia, taking a seat in front of the man's desk while Chase opted to remain standing. "He worked for you, is that correct?"

"Not as an employee," said Mr. Joki, settling in his swivel chair and turning this way and that. "I only use freelancers nowadays. Much more flexible that way. Sometimes you'll have three parties in a single weekend, other times nothing for weeks on end."

"He worked for you as a clown, is that right?" asked Chase.

"Sometimes," said Mr. Joki. "But Justin's big specialty was lookalikes. That's where he really excelled."

"Lookalikes?" asked Odelia.

"Yeah, you know. Someone wants Brad Pitt to come to their party, so they hire a guy who looks like Brad Pitt. Or Elvis or Scarlett Johansson or whatever."

"And Justin could look like Scarlett Johansson if he wanted to?" asked Chase, sounding incredulous.

Mr. Joki laughed. "He was good, but not that good! No, he had a certain range, of course. He had one of those bland faces, you know. The face of an everyman. And with special makeup techniques he could transform into a lot of different characters. He did the voice, too. Mannerisms. He was really good."

"So... he played Brad Pitt and Elvis?"

"Sure. Matt Damon. Tom Cruise. Not Ben Affleck. Different kind of face—more stretched out, if you see what I mean. But all those square-faced guys—Tom Hanks, too."

"Uh-huh," said Chase, clearly surprised.

"I'll bet he could have played you, Detective Kingsley. All he had to do was study you for a while, and listen to the way you talked, and he could slip right into your shoes."

"Amazing," said Odelia.

"Isn't it? Yeah, he might have been a flop on Broadway,

but he was a big hit with the kids. And when he paired up with some of the other lookalikes... Went down a storm." The interview over, Chase and Odelia got up, and so did Mr. Joki. "Say, if you catch the guy who did this, will you let me know? Justin was more than a colleague. He was also my friend."

Once outside, I found Dooley regarding me thoughtfully.

"What is it?" I asked.

"Just wondering if this Justin Troller could have imitated us."

"I doubt it, Dooley. Didn't you hear what the man said? He had to share at least a passing resemblance to the person. And no human bears any resemblance to a cat."

"He also said that he could only imitate square-faced individuals. And you have a square face, Max."

"No, I don't."

"Yes, you do. Definitely square."

Oh, boy.

CHAPTER 29

"So what now?" asked Odelia.

"Now we go back to the office and report to the Chief," said Chase. "And hopefully he'll have an idea what to do next. Cause honestly? Right now I'm pretty much lost, babe."

He drove us all back to the precinct, and we'd just arrived when a man was being led in, valiantly struggling against his restraints, clearly not happy about being arrested.

"We've got him, boss," said one of the officers escorting the man.

"Got who?" asked Chase.

"This is the guy who ran down Vincent Rebela. Isn't that right, tough guy?"

"I'm not saying anything without my lawyer," the man grumbled.

"We caught him on CCTV driving away from the scene in the same make and model the witness saw. And he's got a big dent in his fender. And I'm pretty sure that if we give that fender a closer look, we'll find a match with Rebela's clothes —maybe even blood."

"Great job, Jones," said Chase, clapping the other man on the back.

And while his colleague escorted the man into the station, Jones stayed behind. "You know who that is, don't you?"

"No, who?"

"Brian Scarr. Works for Davide Salvia."

Chase whistled through his teeth.

"Who's Davide Salvia?" I asked.

"Big crime boss," Odelia whispered. "Owns several restaurants, but his real business is loan-sharking, money laundering, drugs… You name it and Salvia has a finger in the pie."

"He likes to stick his fingers in pies?" asked Dooley. "That's not very hygienic."

Jones and Chase had disappeared into the police station, and Odelia also walked through those double doors.

"So why would a well-known crime boss run down Emma van de Graaf's boyfriend?" I asked no one in particular.

"Maybe Emma is a mobster?" Dooley suggested.

"Let's go, Dooley," I said.

"Where are we going?"

"Kingman."

And so we left the precinct, eager for some fresh air, and some crime-free moments. And of course the very best kibble in town, courtesy of Kingman's human Wilbur Vickery.

"Hey, fellas," said Kingman when he saw us walk up. "How are things in the world of mayhem and mystery?"

"Not too good," I confessed.

"We met a fashion designer who likes to design clothes for scarecrows," said Dooley, "and a man who supplies lookalikes, but only for people with square faces. And Emma van de Graaf's boyfriend was run down by a man who likes to stick his fingers in pies."

"Looks like you guys had a busy day," said Kingman, then gestured to his bowl of kibble, located underneath the tomato stand in front of the store. "Dig in. It's a new kind of kibble that Wilbur is trying out. If I like it—or my friends—he'll buy it in bulk."

Wilbur Vickery is always being approached by suppliers who are trying to sell him their wares. It's good for us, of course, since we often get to sample those wares, and give them our seal of approval—or not, as the case may be.

"This is some good stuff, Kingman," I said, my mouth full of the most delicious kibble I'd had in a while. "Very tasty."

"It's excellent," said Dooley. "Better tell Wilbur to buy more of it."

Kingman was smiling like a shopkeeper who sees his customers enjoy his sold goods. "That's the beauty of it. I don't have to tell him anything. If by tonight that bowl is empty, he knows I liked it. If it's not, he knows I hated it. So eat your fill, fellas. There's plenty more where this came from."

Once we'd emptied the bowl, Dooley suddenly said, "I think I've solved the case, Max."

"What case?" I asked. "Cause it looks to me as if we're dealing with just about a hundred different cases right now."

"The case of the murdered business tycoon," Dooley said. "I think the Mafia is involved."

"The Mafia, huh? How do you figure that?"

"Just look at that bug Emma found in her apartment, and her boyfriend almost being killed by that mobster. I think the Mafia paid Emma to steal all of that Nazi art, and now they're trying to silence her by running down Vincent." He nodded seriously. "It's a warning, Max. The Mafia always gives a warning before they do anything."

"Don't they usually put the head of a horse in somebody's bed?" asked Kingman.

"They probably ran out of horses, so they had to try something different."

"Mh," I said, not convinced.

"Say, you're right. This stuff is pretty good," said Kingman, who was sampling a few nuggets of the new kibble himself now. "I think I'd like Wilbur to order more."

"Must be nice when you have a human who has his own shop," I said. "And he can order you any kibble you like, and any wet food. Or even fresh fish and meats aplenty."

"Yeah, nobody tells Wilbur what to buy," said Kingman. "He's like the ruler of his own domain. You should see the number of suppliers who come knocking on his door—or call him at all hours of the day. All of them trying to get him to carry their stuff. But at the end of the day, it's Wilbur's business, and if he buys something that his customers don't like, he loses money."

"Yeah, I guess it must be hard to distinguish between the crooks and the bona fide sellers," I said.

"Oh, absolutely. You wouldn't believe the kind of junk he gets offered."

"Okay, so if it wasn't the Mafia," said Dooley, "how about the government?"

I arched an eyebrow at him.

"Bear with me, Max. That bug is bugging me, all right?"

"It's bugging me, too," I said.

"What bug?" asked Kingman.

"Emma van de Graaf found a bug in her apartment."

"So? She should get pest control out there."

"Not that kind of bug."

"Okay, so the government planted that bug, see?" said Dooley. "Because they wanted her to steal all that Nazi art!"

"What Nazi art?" asked Kingman.

"Emma was John Robie," I explained. "And she stole all of

that art to give it back to the people it was originally taken from. By the Nazis."

"I don't like Nazis," said Kingman. "All that beer and sauerkraut. Bad taste."

"Okay, so the government trained her to become a stealing machine," said Dooley, "because they wanted to get their hands on all of that art. Only Emma disagreed and now they're putting her under pressure by trying to kill her boyfriend."

"I don't think the government would try and kill people's boyfriends, Dooley," I said. "And also, even if they did, they would use their own trained assassins, not a mob enforcer."

"You think so?"

"Yes, Dooley. So try again, cause this theory of yours doesn't cut wood."

"Nazi art, hit-and-runs, mobster enforcers—what case did you guys get mixed up in this time?" said Kingman, shaking his head.

"A complicated case," I said. "In fact a real head-scratcher."

And to show Kingman that my words held merit, Dooley scratched his head right then.

"I'm officially stumped, Max," my friend declared. "The only thing I know for sure is that if only these people would take up golf instead of going around trying to kill each other, we wouldn't be faced with this problem!"

"Wise words, Dooley," I said with a tolerant smile.

CHAPTER 30

We were back at the hospital, where we found Emma still guarding her boyfriend, not moving from his side.

"We've got some news for you, Emma," said Odelia, taking a seat next to the woman. "We caught the man who ran over Vincent."

"You did? Oh, that's great news."

"Turns out he works for a local crime boss," said Chase, studying Emma's face closely as he spoke these words.

Her face only showed surprise. "A crime boss? I don't understand."

"We think your boyfriend wasn't run over by accident," said Odelia. "We think he was deliberately targeted."

"Only we have no idea why," said Chase. "Would you know why Vincent was on the hit list of a local crime syndicate?"

Emma shook her head, looking puzzled. "No, I have no idea. Vincent is a schoolteacher. He's not involved with organized crime at all."

"What about you?" asked Chase. "In your capacity as John Robie, were you ever contacted by these people?"

"No. I already explained to you why we burgled those places. All we wanted was to steal artwork that had been stolen in the first place, and return it to its rightful owners."

"Okay, so how about this," said Chase, as he paced the floor. "Brian Scarr's bosses—"

"Brian Scarr? Is he the man who…"

"Yes, he's the person who was involved in the hit-and-run," said Odelia.

"So Mr. Scarr's bosses somehow discover the identity of John Robie," Chase continued. "Naturally they're most interested in laying their hands on that artwork, which is worth a great deal of money. So they start keeping tabs on you and Vincent. They bug your apartment. They're planning to move in on you once you've pulled enough burglaries. Only your grandfather gets killed and the murder weapon points to you. So they get cold feet and pull out. And in that case this hit-and-run is their way of getting even."

"I don't know, Detective Kingsley," said Emma. "All I can tell you is that I've never had anything to do with these people." Odelia now showed her a picture of Mr. Scarr and she shook her head. "No, I've never seen him before in my life."

"We also spoke to your brother's husband," said Odelia, "and it turns out he's being faced with some financial difficulties. I think Royce and Jeff were really counting on a windfall in case your grandfather died, and now it turns out that isn't going to happen."

"I know. My parents and Casey were here. They told me what happened."

"Did your brother know about you being John Robie?" asked Chase.

Emma shook her head. "No. I didn't tell anyone. Not even Casey, even though we've always been close. I didn't want to put her in a difficult position in case I was caught."

"And what about your relationship with Royce?"

"I love my brother very much, but we've never been very close."

"So he definitely didn't know that you stole that dagger?" asked Odelia.

"No, as far as I know he had no way of knowing."

"One more thing, Emma, and then we'll leave you in peace," said Chase. "Do you think either your brother or Jeff are capable of stealing that dagger, then murdering your grandfather and incriminating you in the process?"

"No, of course not. My brother and I may not be close, but he would never do that to me. Also, Royce isn't capable of murder."

"He does have a quick temper," Odelia pointed out.

"Yes, but that doesn't make him a killer."

"And how about Jeff Malkan?" asked Chase.

"Absolutely not. Jeff is an artist. A sensitive and creative soul. He's not a murderer."

Both Chase and Odelia looked disappointed. They weren't getting anywhere like this.

Just then, the door swung open and a man walked in carrying a large bouquet of flowers. I recognized him as Guy Batozy, restaurateur and Emma's ex-boyfriend.

When he caught sight of Chase and Odelia, he hesitated for a moment, then went ahead and offered the bouquet to Emma. "I heard about what happened," he said. "I wanted to tell you that if there's anything you need, anything at all, you just have to say the word."

"Thanks, Guy," said Emma. "That's very kind of you."

"Well," said Guy, dancing from one leg to the other, and obviously not having expected to find Emma in the presence of company, "I guess I'll, um… Well, if you need anything…"

"Yes," she said. "Thanks."

"Is he… Will he…"

Emma shook her head. "The doctor said that all we can do now is wait—and pray. They've done all they can."

Guy nodded. "Terrible business," he murmured. "Came as soon as I heard." He gave Emma a final nod, then walked out again.

She directed a curious look at the door. "Odd," she said. "It's the first time I've spoken to Guy since we broke up."

"He seemed nervous," said Odelia.

"He's always been a little tongue-tied around me," said Emma with a smile. "I seem to have that effect on him. I remember our first date. He practically didn't say a word. I had to carry the conversation all through dinner."

"And you still ended up dating him?"

"He was a nice change of pace from my usual type of boyfriend. Not as brash and uber-confident, you know. More quiet and timid. I loved that about him. But then I met Vincent, and that was like a bolt from the blue. You hear so much about love at first sight, and I always thought it was a ridiculous concept, but that was what happened when I saw Vincent for the first time. And so I broke up with Guy."

"You broke up with Guy? He told us he broke up with you," said Odelia.

"Typical guy talk. They can't admit defeat, can they? So of course he's the one who ended it. No, the moment I met Vincent I knew I wanted to spend my life with him." She pressed Vincent's hand in both of hers and tears sprung to her eyes afresh. "I just hope he pulls through. He has to. He just has to."

"Do you think Guy could be involved in this murder business, Max?" asked Dooley.

"I doubt it, Dooley," I said. "The man has an ironclad alibi. He was in the kitchen of his restaurant at the time of the murder, and was seen by dozens of people."

"Too bad," said Dooley. "Because if he didn't do it, or

Royden, or Abisha, or Royce, or Royce's husband, then that only leaves Emma. And I like Emma, Max!"

"Yeah, I like her, too," I said, glancing up at the young woman, who was clinging to the love of her life with such fervor.

CHAPTER 31

We finally found ourselves on familiar territory again: home! It had been a long day, and frankly I couldn't wait to curl up into a ball on my favorite couch and do some napping—and thinking, of course.

This case was really baffling, and I wanted to take the time to make all those puzzle pieces floating around in my head settle down into a—hopefully—neat pattern.

But before I could do that, Harriet and Brutus wanted to have speech with me.

"Why hasn't anyone been arrested yet?" Harriet demanded heatedly. "I already told you who did it, and still the person hasn't been arrested."

"You said the ghost of the socialist butler did it," I pointed out. "It's very hard to arrest a ghost, Harriet, even a socialist ghost. They're too ephemeral to pin down. Also, they tend to escape by floating through the bars of their prison cell."

"Oh, don't be such a smart-ass, Max. When I said butler of course I meant any member of the household staff. Whether it was the butler or the maid or the cook is semantics."

"So now you think the cook did it, do you?"

"Exactly! But you'll find that it was in fact a conspiracy. They're all in on it! But of course one of them had to wield the knife, and I think you'll agree with me that the cook is the most likely person for the job. After all, a cook is used to handling knives."

"I like your theory," I said, "but I doubt whether Odelia will agree with you. Or Chase."

"We'll see about that," she said defiantly.

"Hey, sugar lips," said Brutus, slipping in through the cat flap, "Dooley says an arrest has been made."

Harriet snapped her head around so fast I could have sworn I heard a creaking sound. "I thought no one had been arrested yet!"

"Not in the Rudyard van de Graaf murder case," I said. "But in the hit-and-run case of Vincent Rebela a man has indeed been arrested."

"What hit-and-run? What are you talking about?"

"Emma's boyfriend was hit by a car," Dooley explained. He'd also slipped in through the cat flap, and was clearly eager to add his two cents to the conversation. "But I think it was the government, punishing him for not handing over that stolen Nazi art."

"Dooley, shut up," said Harriet. "Okay, so it's pretty obvious, isn't it? The cook, after she killed Rudyard van de Graaf, decided to silence any potential witnesses, so she's on a murderous rampage now. First she killed Vincent, and the next one on her list is Emma."

"Vincent is still alive," I pointed out. "He survived the attempt on his life. And also, the man arrested for the crime is an enforcer for a well-known local crime boss."

Harriet frowned, and I could see her little gray cells working feverishly to fit this into her theory. "Okay," she said slowly, "so the cook obviously has to cook, so she ordered a hit online. Anyone can order a hit online these days. Easy peasy."

"Oh, and then there is that actor who was killed," said Dooley. "But I don't think that's connected to the first murder at all."

"What actor?" Harriet demanded.

"A man who used to play a clown at kids' parties and who worked as a lookalike was killed this afternoon," I said. "His house was burgled and he was murdered, probably by the burglar."

"Well, that's what happens when you don't pay attention to the opinion of an ace sleuth like me," she said, tilting her chin. "If only Odelia and Chase had consulted me, they could have solved the first murder, and the second murder could have been avoided."

"I'm not following you," I confessed.

"Isn't it obvious? Chase and Odelia are spending all of their time looking for Rudyard van de Graaf's killer. If only they had more time on their hands, they could have spent it preventing crime instead of solving it. Basic logic, Max. And now if there's nothing else, I'm going to lie down for a while. My little gray cells need some rest. I've been working them too hard already." She placed a paw to her head and murmured, "I suddenly feel faint. Brutus, take me away, please. I will be alone."

"Of course, tootsie roll," said Brutus, and led his beloved up the stairs, where she could have a lie-down on Odelia and Chase's bed.

"Tough, being an ace sleuth," said Dooley as he stared after the twosome.

"Yeah, pretty tough," I said.

And then I finally gave myself up to thought—allowing my own little gray cells to put in some hard work. Of course, as everyone knows, the best way to exercise that formidable brain of ours is to simply allow it some time to switch off.

And so I lay myself down on the couch… and promptly dozed off.

It must have been close to midnight when I suddenly woke up from a deep sleep. And the moment I did, suddenly the whole thing clicked into place, just like a jigsaw puzzle.

"Of course," I said. "Why didn't I see it sooner!"

And immediately I went in search of Odelia.

I just hoped it wasn't too late!

CHAPTER 32

Guy Batozy, like many men in their forties, had acquired a morning routine over the years of which he never varied. Before he got up, he visualized for a few moments the day as it stretched out before him in all its glorious detail. His business kept expanding, expanding, expanding. His health kept increasing, increasing, increasing. His wealth kept growing, growing, growing…

And of course he also pictured himself getting closer and closer to the ideal he'd set himself as a young man: a wealthy, successful restaurateur with a booming business but also a great home life, a loving wife waiting in the wings, and several young Batozys darting about.

He smiled as he swung his feet to the floor, then immediately spread out his pink yoga mat and launched into his daily practice. His muscles sufficiently warmed up, he mounted his cross trainer and put in forty minutes of a grueling workout, making sure he kept that middle-aged body of his free from flab and as well-conserved as humanly possible.

A refreshing shower took care of all that honest fitness

PURRFECT THIEF

sweat, and then it was finally time for the first highlight of the day: a breakfast for champions, consisting of plenty of fruits, nuts and grains.

The hitch in his routine came when he grabbed the Hampton Cove Gazette, the newspaper he liked to peruse while enjoying his breakfast.

'Listening devices were found in the apartment of prominent family scion Emma van de Graaf. "Who is spying on us?" Emma demands to know.'

'Police announce they're ready to make an arrest in the van de Graaf murder case.'

'Well-known mob enforcer was arrested yesterday.'

He sat back and gave himself up to a moment of thought, then read through the article about the enforcer. A few snippets immediately jumped out at him: *'Brian Scarr is fully cooperating with the police, providing valuable information about his client.'*

Guy gulped a little. Suddenly his breakfast didn't taste as well as it usually did.

'The police have announced that they're following several lines of inquiry after Scarr's full confession. Further arrests are imminent.'

Suddenly experiencing an attack of nausea, Guy pushed himself away from the kitchen counter and walked over to the window. Since he lived above his own restaurant, he was in the habit of looking out at the entrance below, to see whether customers were already lining up. Today, however, he wasn't interested in how many customers were eager to take breakfast in his establishment. Instead, he scanned the street for signs of the strong arm of the law.

More snippets from the morning edition of the Gazette now flashed through his mind.

'According to police sources the motive for the van de Graaf murder is revenge.'

'Vincent Rebela, victim of a hit-and-run, regains consciousness. He's expected to make a full recovery.'

Beads of sweat were now standing out across the restaurant owner's brow and he inserted a finger between neck and collar. To no avail, however, as that feeling of nausea only increased.

And then suddenly he became aware of a flashing blue light reflecting across the ceiling of his apartment and he uttered a startled cry.

He quickly returned to the window, and lo and behold: that cop Chase Kingsley, along with his wife, were standing down below, looking up at him... and waving!

And judging from the shit-eating grin on the burly cop's face, and the fact that his hand was fondling a pair of shiny handcuffs, suddenly gave the restaurant owner the kind of shock usually reserved for people unexpectedly struck by lightning.

In full panic mode now, he didn't think—he ran. He opened the sliding glass door that led out onto the balcony at the back of his apartment, then started shimmying down the drainpipe. He landed on the flat roof of the restaurant kitchen and hurried in the direction of the back. If he could make it out the back entrance, he was safe. He had a car parked on the adjacent street, and...

Much to his consternation, three police officers approached him from that exact back entrance. He turned to the front, and was about to step into the kitchen, when Mr. and Mrs. Kingsley joined him from that side.

Oh, God. He was for it now, wasn't he?

"Mr. Guy Batozy," said the lanky detective, "you're under arrest for the murder of Rudyard van de Graaf, conspiracy to commit murder on Justin Troller, and conspiracy for the attempted murder of Vincent Rebela."

"How did you find out?" he asked, slightly out of breath now. "It's that idiot Scarr, isn't it? He told you."

"I think you better come with us, Mr. Batozy," said Detective Kingsley.

And so he came, meekly and with all the air of a man who knew that he was licked.

"I should have done it myself," he muttered. "Everyone knows that if you want a job done well you better do it yourself."

"You have the right to remain silent, Mr. Batozy," the detective reminded him, but Guy wasn't the kind of person who liked to remain silent.

"I was trying to be clever, you know. I should have just killed him and got it over with. Much easier. But no, I had to be the smart one. Well, look where it brought me."

"Killed Vincent?" asked Odelia Kingsley.

He nodded. "But I couldn't, could I? Stupid, stupid, stupid."

He glanced at his kitchen staff, who all looked completely stunned as their boss was being led past them in handcuffs.

"What's going to happen to my restaurant now?" he asked. "Who's going to run it?"

But it was obvious that no answer was forthcoming. The restaurant would go to the bank, who'd sell it and probably turn it into a pizza parlor or a kebab place.

"Oh, hell and damnation!" he cried, and then was shoved into a police car, his head pushed down to make sure he didn't slam it into the doorframe.

EPILOGUE

"Guy Batozy was indeed dumped by Emma van de Graaf, even though he liked to claim it was the other way around. Emma didn't like his domineering ways, and had the impression that the only reason he was interested in her was as a potential investor in his restaurant business."

"He saw her as a meal ticket," Harriet said.

"Exactly," I said. "And she resented that."

The four of us were sitting on the porch swing, as is our habit, while the human contingent were gathered for that weekly ritual: the backyard barbecue. Tex was making a valiant attempt to provide his nearest and dearest with a full array of nutritious food, assisted in his endeavors by not one but two helpers: Chase and Uncle Alec. It was the only way to make sure that stomachs wouldn't go empty and appetites were satisfied.

Gran and Scarlett were explaining to anyone who would listen how they had resumed their patrols, since someone had to keep those mean streets of our town safe from crime, and Odelia was explaining to her mom and to Charlene how she and Chase had managed to collar

Rudyard van de Graaf's killer, with a little help from yours truly.

"I don't get it," said Dooley. "I thought Mr. Batozy had an alibi for the murder?"

"He did, and he'd worked hard to supply himself with it. But in actual fact the murder didn't take place around four, but one hour earlier, around three o'clock."

"But I thought Rudyard van de Graaf was fitting a new suit at three o'clock?" asked Brutus.

"That wasn't Rudyard. That was Justin Troller, dressed up and made to look like Rudyard. You see, Guy had hired him for that particular job, presumably telling him that Rudyard himself didn't like to go out and about anymore, due to his advanced age, but that Justin had about the same build and height as the old man, so he was selected to go to Giuseppe Tallett and get fitted for that suit. And since Rudyard had never been a customer there, the tailor didn't know that he was actually fitting Justin Troller for a new suit."

"Is that why Justin was killed?" asked Dooley.

I nodded. "Guy couldn't risk having any witnesses, so he hired Brian Scarr, a well-known organized crime enforcer, to get rid of Justin, and make it look like a burglary. He knew Scarr through Scarr's boss Davide Salvia, who's also in the restaurant business."

"But why? Why did Guy want to kill Rudyard?" asked Harriet, who looked thoroughly puzzled.

"Because Guy wanted to get even with Emma. Not only had she unceremoniously dumped him, which had been a great blow to his ego, but all the plans he had made to build a chain of restaurants with van de Graaf money went up in smoke when she did. You see, he'd already envisioned a future for himself as Emma's husband, a future where he was a real mover and shaker, and would become the person he always wanted to be: a top restaurateur, not just the owner of one local restaurant but of a nationwide chain. And so when Emma broke up with him, he saw all his hopes and dreams go down the drain."

"And so he killed her grandfather and tried to put the blame on her," said Brutus.

"Exactly. Though I think the man was actually in love with her, and when she dumped him, he was truly heartbroken. She became an obsession with him. So he broke into the apartment she shared with Vincent and bugged the place, so he could spy on the couple."

When the police had searched Guy's flat, they'd found plenty of evidence that he'd been spying on Emma and Vincent for months. They'd also found a duplicate key of Emma's apartment, one he made when they were still dating, and which he kept.

"Poor man," said Dooley. "He really lost it, didn't he?"

"He did," I confirmed. "And when he discovered that Emma and Vincent were burgling the houses of her parents' rich friends, an idea must have formed in his mind. He would implicate her in a murder, and in doing so break her spirit. Then he'd have her boyfriend killed and be there for her when she was at her lowest ebb and win her back somehow."

"Sounds pretty delusional to me," said Harriet.

"The day of the murder he broke into the apartment again, to remove all the bugs, since he knew the police would search her place once they discovered Emma's fingerprints on the Drossart Dagger, and also took the dagger. Then he set up his alibi. He'd hired Justin Troller to pretend to be Rudyard. Guy knew his way around the van de Graaf mansion, and he knew all about the secret passageways, and since he had an excuse for hanging around the house, with him catering Rudyard's upcoming birthday bash, he snuck out of the kitchen that afternoon, up to Rudyard's apartment, killed the old man with the dagger and left it there. Then he snuck out again and drove back to the restaurant and made sure he was seen by plenty of people. And since the police would think that Rudyard had been killed at four o'clock, and not at three, he was in the clear."

"But why run down Vincent?" asked Dooley.

"Because he saw Vincent as the reason Emma broke up with him. So the man had to die. He hoped that once Vincent was dead, he could win Emma back. Unfortunately for him Scarr didn't do a good job, and on top of that managed to get himself arrested."

"Did Scarr really confess and finger Guy Batozy as his client?" asked Brutus.

I smiled. "No, he didn't. But I suggested that Odelia write an article claiming he was fully cooperating with the police. She also wrote about the bugs they found."

"Bug, singular," Harriet corrected me. "Guy must have forgotten one, right?"

"Yeah, he did. One of his mistakes. The articles made sure he was on edge, and then when he saw Chase and Odelia show up, he ran, and in doing so admitted his guilt."

"Clever," said Harriet.

"So how about the message that Emma received from her grandfather?" asked Brutus. "Telling her to meet him?"

"That message was sent by Guy, of course, with a disposable phone. He wanted to make sure that Emma had no alibi for the murder, placing her at the scene of the crime."

"What a devious man," said Dooley.

"Yeah, and if we hadn't caught him, I'm sure he was going to set up another attempt on Vincent's life. The man just had to die. That's why he was at the hospital, offering Emma a bouquet of flowers. He wanted to stake out the place—figure out how to finish Vince off."

"But how did you figure it out?" asked Harriet.

"I wondered about that suit. Why would a man who ran

his family and his business with an iron fist feel the need to sneak around their back to have a new suit made? It seemed so out of character for Rudyard. And that's because he didn't have a suit made. At the time the fake Rudyard was being fitted for a suit, the real Rudyard was already dead. Also: it takes four to six weeks for a bespoke suit to be made, so why start the process one week before your birthday? And then once I started thinking some more about this whole suit business, it wasn't a big leap to Justin Troller, the square-faced lookalike. Square-faced, just like the van de Graaf patriarch. Also, according to his neighbor he hadn't entered the house when he'd arrived with the cab, but had taken a stroll. Which is obvious once you know that he was in fact Justin: he couldn't very well walk in through the front door. And then of course there were the discrepancies in Emma and Guy's statements about who had ended their affair and Brian Scarr's connection to the restaurant business. All the pieces of the puzzle finally fell into place at that point."

"Good thinking, Max," said Brutus, offering me a rare compliment.

"Of course I knew all along that Guy Batozy was the killer," said Harriet, flicking an imaginary piece of lint from her coat of fur.

"I thought you said the ghost of the butler did it?" I said. "Or the cook?"

"That was just to test you, Max. I figured it out long before you did, but I decided to give you a chance." She offered me a smile. "I have to say it took you long enough. I really thought you would have figured it out much sooner."

Brutus was eyeing her strangely, but when she looked over to him, he quickly nodded. "Oh, yes, of course. We figured it out a long time ago. And then it was just a waiting game, to see if Max would catch up with us or not."

"Of course," I said good-naturedly. Yes, I was in a good

mood. Wouldn't you be? I'd helped my human catch a nasty killer, I'd had a good helping of delicious food, and now that Guy Batozy was in jail, I'd finally caught up on my sleep. So Harriet could say whatever she wanted, it didn't faze me.

"So what's going to happen to the van de Graafs?" asked Brutus. "Is Casey going to run the family business from now on?"

"I think they're all going to keep running it the way they've done for a while now," I said. "With Royden, Abisha, Royce, Casey and Emma all pulling together and trying to lift the business out of the slump it has found itself in. And now that Rudyard is gone, I'm convinced relations between the family members are going to improve vastly."

"Rudyard did seem to like to play one against the other," said Dooley.

"Yes, he did. He believed in divide and conquer, but that's no way to run a family business. And also, from what I've heard, a merger is being discussed, between the van de Graafs and the Mulhearns. Casey and Zalman may not be prepared to get married, but they are more than happy to get in bed together—in a business sense, that is."

"Good for them," said Dooley. "I like Casey and I like Zalman. I think they'll do great things."

"Yeah, I think so, too."

For a moment, we were all quiet as we enjoyed the aftermath of a good meal. Then Harriet suddenly piped up, "You know, Max? I've been thinking."

"Mh?" I said, feeling a little sleepy.

"With Casey and Zalman pooling their strengths, they'll probably make a success of things, right?"

"Oh, absolutely," I said. "They're very smart, those two."

"So what would happen if an admittedly clever detective like you teams up with a master sleuth like me? I think we could do some real damage, don't you think?"

I glanced over to Harriet, wondering what she was up to this time. "I guess so," I said, a little guardedly.

"So what do you say, Max?"

"About what?"

"About you and me working together."

"But… I thought that was what we've been doing all along."

"Yeah, I know, but this time for real."

"Um…"

She rolled her eyes. "Oh, God. For a smart cat you really aren't all that smart, are you? I want us to be a team from now on. You and I will be in charge, of course, and Dooley and Brutus will be our sidekicks. Brutus provides the brute force, Dooley provides…" She studied Dooley for a moment. "Well, something. And together the four of us will be unbeatable."

I gave her an indulgent smile. "So what's the catch?"

"No catch. I just think it's silly for us to be in competition. Cooperation is key. The whole is greater than the sum of its parts and all that. So the sum of four makes five, or even six or seven."

"I don't think the sum of four is five," said Dooley. "Is it?"

I glanced over to Brutus, who gave me a surreptitious nod.

"You're the brains of this outfit, Max," he said.

"Well…" Harriet said.

"I'm the muscle and Harriet is the beauty."

"That's true," Harriet admitted.

"And me?" asked Dooley. "What am I?"

Brutus stared at him. "Can I get back to you on that, Dooley?"

"Dooley is the glue that holds it all together," suddenly Harriet said. "Without Dooley, this…" She gestured between the four of us. "Wouldn't work. So you have a very important role to play, Dooley."

"Really?" asked Dooley, his face lighting up.

"Really," said Harriet with a smile, and gave the gray Ragamuffin a peck on the cheek, which made him blush under his fur. Possibly it even made him forget Minnie.

"Okay," I said. "Let's work together from now on."

"Great," said Harriet. "Now I was thinking we'd call ourselves Harriet's Outfit. Or maybe Harriet's Crew? Or how about Harriet's Detective Agency? Or how about…"

She had more suggestions to make, but I was long overdue on my next nap, and so I put my head on my paws and prepared to doze off.

"Harriet's Flunkies? No, that doesn't have the right ring to it. Harriet's Angels? Or no, I've got it! Harriet's Gumshoes!"

"What's a gumshoe, Harriet?" asked Dooley. "Is that like gum on your shoe?"

"Oh, Dooley…"

THE END

Thanks for reading! If you want to know when a new Nic Saint book comes out, sign up for Nic's mailing list: nicsaint.com/news

EXCERPT FROM PURRFECT CRUST (THE MYSTERIES OF MAX 44)

Chapter One

It was one of those lazy days where nothing happens and where all you can do is take prolonged naps and do nothing in particular. In other words: exactly my kind of day!

Dooley and I were in Odelia's office, napping and generally have a relaxing time. In fact it isn't too much to say that the only one putting in a day's labor was Odelia herself, typing away on her laptop on an article about a recent hayride that had turned into a joyride when a group of kids had stolen a car and managed to wreck it and the chicken coop they'd mowed down.

Environmentalists and vegetarians alike had screamed bloody murder, as had the owners of—respectively—the car and the chicken coop.

In other words: just another summer in the Hamptons.

And the day would have passed uneventfully, as any perfect day does, if not a young woman had suddenly walked into the office, clearly in something of a turmoil, judging from her worried expression, which told me she was facing some terrible ordeal.

I wondered for a moment if she, too, had had a chicken coop demolished, but for some reason she didn't look like a chicken coop owner, and so I pricked up my ears, and waited for her to launch into speech, which she promptly did.

"Mrs. Kingsley? Dan Goory sent me. He says you have a knack for dealing with delicate problems."

Odelia looked up from her article and smiled a reassuring smile at the woman.

"Take a seat," she suggested. "You're friends with Dan?"

The woman took the proffered seat and shook her head. "My mother knows Dan well. She actually suggested I talk to him, and he sent me to you."

"And you are…"

"Oh, I'm sorry. Where are my manners. My name is Sasha Kay. I don't know if you know Arlette Kay? She's my mom."

"I don't think I've had the pleasure," said Odelia.

Mrs. Kay was dressed in jeans and a gray sweater, and her flaming red hair was tied back from a high forehead in a bun. She was pale and had lots of freckles and the most striking green eyes.

"She's very pretty, isn't she, Max?" said Dooley, who'd also woken up.

"Yes, she is," I agreed. "And also very nervous."

"Most people who visit Odelia are nervous," said my friend. "I wonder why that is. She's not a very scary person, is she?"

"No, she's not, but the people who visit her are usually in some kind of trouble."

It's true. In a very short time Odelia has become the go-to person in this town for troubled souls. All of them turn to her to find a solution for what ails them. And you know what? Oftentimes she manages to help them out. In fact her success rate is probably higher than most private investigators. But then she's a very clever person, Odelia is.

"What seems to be the problem?" she asked now, intertwining her fingers on the desk and offering Sasha Kay her full attention.

"I've been fired from my job," said Mrs. Kay.

"Where do you work?"

"At Saker's Bakers on Stanwyck Street."

"Oh, I know Saker's Bakers. My grandmother goes there all the time. They have the best pastry."

Mrs. Kay smiled a watery smile. "They have. I work behind the counter, you see, and a couple of weeks ago my little boy was sick, and I didn't have enough money to pay the hospital. So I took a hundred dollars from the till, knowing I'd get my paycheck a week later, and could return the money then. But when I did return the money, Mrs. Saker, that's the baker's wife, caught me and wanted to know what I was doing. So I explained to her about the hospital, and she said it was all right for once."

"That was very kind of her."

"It was. She's not a bad person, only she can be very strict sometimes. And then last week suddenly five hundred dollars suddenly went missing from the till, and of course Mrs. Saker remembered that time when she caught me and accused me of stealing."

"And did you? Take the money?"

"No! Of course not. But she told her husband, and he immediately called the police and fired me on the spot, even though I tried to explain to him that it had just been an emergency that time, and I'd promised never to do it again. Only he doesn't believe me."

"So who do you think took the money this time?"

"I don't know, but I suspect Mrs. Saker herself. I've seen her on more than one occasion take money from the cash register, but then of course she's the owner, so it's her money. But I'm pretty sure Mr. Saker doesn't know."

"And you think she took it and very conveniently put the blame on you."

Sasha Kay nodded. She was on the verge of tears now, and was having a hard time hanging on to her composure. "I need that job, Mrs. Kingsley. I really do."

"Odelia, please, Mrs. Kay."

She gave a feeble smile. "Sasha."

"What did the police say?"

"They were only in there five minutes. Mrs. Saker said they'd made a mistake and would arrange things themselves. Which is why I think that she took the money and doesn't want the police to look too closely at what happened."

"Is there a camera in the shop?"

Sasha shook her head. "No. It's just a small shop, and Damien Saker, that's the baker, runs his business on a basis of trust. I've worked there five years now, and never had any trouble before. But he said some very harsh things to me. Said I'd betrayed his trust, and had stabbed him in the back with my underhanded behavior. He said that if I really needed that money I could have talked to him and he could have arranged a loan. But when I told him I didn't do it he said that my lies hurt him more than my thieving. I tried to speak to him alone, to tell him that I suspected his wife, but Edwina wouldn't allow it."

"Which is exactly the kind of thing a guilty person would do," said Odelia musingly.

"Look, I need that job. I'm a single mother and already it's hard enough for me to make ends meet. And with this accusation hanging over my head, no other store in town will hire me. Already Edwina has been going around telling people that I'm a thief and a liar."

"That's bad," said Odelia with a frown.

"It is. Not only has she falsely accused me of something I didn't do, but now she's trying to destroy my reputation and my future."

"Do you want me to go and talk to Damien Saker? Try to make him see your side of things?"

"Oh, please could you? He won't listen to me, but maybe he'll listen to you."

"I can always try," said Odelia, giving the stricken woman a reassuring smile.

"The problem is that Damien is crazy about his wife, so even if she confesses about taking that money, I'm not sure he'll take me back, since he'd lose face and so would she."

"Yeah, and it might not be possible for you and Edwina to work together after what happened."

"But I still want her to own up to what she did. And I want her to stop spreading lies about me."

"What I don't understand is why Edwina would steal from her own shop. After all, it's her money."

Sasha shook her head. "There's a rumor that Edwina has a hole in her hand, and that Damien has taken away her credit cards and has blocked access to their account at the bank. There have been some flaming rows lately."

"I see."

"The woman owns more dresses and shoes than I've owned in my entire life. And still she keeps on buying more. The bakery is doing well, but they're not making Rockefeller money. And definitely not enough to pay for Edwina's shopping addiction."

"Yeah, that would explain why she felt the need to take money from the till." Odelia got up. "You know what? I'll go over there right now, and talk to Damien. And I'm sure that things can be ironed out very easily."

"Oh, thank you," said Sasha, and this time tears actually

did spring to her eyes. "I don't have a lot of money to pay you, but…"

"That's all right," said Odelia. "If I'm not mistaken there just might be a good story in there somewhere."

Sasha smiled through her tears. "Dan said as much."

Odelia gave me a pointed look.

"Looks like the peace and calm is over, Dooley," I said.

"Oh, goodie," said my friend. "Do you know I was getting bored just lying here doing nothing, Max?"

I wasn't, but when duty calls…

Chapter Two

We were in luck: when we arrived at Saker's Bakers, the eponymous baker was behind the counter, conferring with his wife and chatting amiably with the customers in the shop. It's not often that you can find a baker putting in an appearance in his own bakery, since these people have to get up at an ungodly hour to get busy baking, and so by the time things get busy in the shop, they're pretty much ready to go to bed.

"Mr. Saker, could I have a word in private, please?" asked Odelia, after introducing herself.

Damien Saker was a short, chunky man, with a thinning mane and small, black eyes. He was the nervy type, as evidenced by a certain quickness of movement and speech.

"Yes, of course," he said, and followed us outside, where we could conduct a conversation out of earshot of both the man's wife and his customers. "Is the Gazette doing an article on my shop?" he asked, rubbing his hands. "Cause that would be most appreciated. We're celebrating fifty years of Saker's Bakers this year, you see, which would make a great topic for a feature story, don't you think?"

"I'm not here to write an article about your bakery, Mr. Saker," said Odelia.

"Oh?" he said, eyes narrowing.

"I'm actually here to talk about Sasha Kay."

Immediately the man's expression darkened. "I don't want to talk about her," he said.

"Sasha didn't take that money, Mr. Saker," said Odelia, not beating about the bush.

"It's her word against my wife's, and you'll understand that I'm more inclined to believe my wife than a woman who's been known to lie before."

"What do you mean?"

"It's not the first time she took money."

"That was different. She needed that money to pay the hospital. And she put it back as soon as she could."

The baker made a scoffing sound. "A likely story. Look, she took money then, and she took money now. And since she got away with it the first time, she thought she could play us for suckers. But this time I'm not having it. She's lucky I'm not pressing charges and having her arrested."

"But your wife has been spreading gossip about her. Ruining her reputation and making it impossible for her to find another job."

The baker shrugged. "I'm sorry, but Sasha brought this on herself, and if Edwina wants to warn certain colleagues of ours about Sasha's thieving ways, that's her business."

"Don't you think you should give Sasha the benefit of the doubt, Mr. Saker? She swears that she didn't take that money."

"Then who did? The Holy Ghost? Somebody took that five hundred from the cash register, Mrs. Kingsley, and she was the only one in the shop that day, apart from Edwina, of course."

Odelia cocked a meaningful eyebrow.

"Oh, I see," said the baker with a tight grin. "She's pointing the finger at my wife. Well, Edwina didn't do it. She doesn't have to! It's our business and she doesn't have to steal."

"It's been said that your wife has a shopping addiction, and that you took away her credit cards. So maybe she needed the money to satisfy that addiction."

The baker gave Odelia a not-so-friendly look. "I think we're done here, Mrs. Kingsley." And he stomped back into his store.

Odelia sighed. "Looks like I could have handled that with just a little bit more diplomacy, you guys."

"You did your best," said Dooley.

"He's a tough egg," I said.

"So what now?" said Odelia.

I glanced up and saw that a 'for hire' poster had been taped to the window. I pointed to the poster and said, "Now you make sure you fill that position with a person you can trust."

Odelia studied the sign for a moment. "Yeah, but who? I can't do it, since he'll never hire me after what happened just now. And also, he knows who I am."

"So how about Gran?" I suggested.

A slow smile curved Odelia's lips. "Now there's an idea…"

We'd arrived at the doctor's office run by Odelia's dad Tex when Gran came storming out.

"I've had it up to here!" the old lady exclaimed as she stood fuming on the sidewalk.

"What's wrong?" asked Odelia.

"Ida Baumgartner, that's what! She keeps filling my head with all kinds of nonsense. Every day she discovers some new and rare disease she claims to suffer from. It's too much!"

"Well, if you need a change of pace, I've got just the thing for you, Gran," said Odelia, as she placed an arm around her grandmother's shoulder. "How would you feel about working at a bakery?"

"Ooh, I'd love that," said Gran. "What bakery?"

"Saker's Bakers."

"I love Saker's Bakers! They've got the best pastry in town. Have you tried their cinnamon apple cake? It's to die for."

"Well, they're hiring right now, so if you go over there you might get lucky."

Gran gave Odelia a curious look. "What's the catch?"

"The catch is that you'll be spying for me."

"That's even better!"

And so in a few words Odelia proceeded to explain to her grandmother what predicament Sasha Kay faced, and how she was hoping to rectify the situation.

"So you want me to get proof that Edwina Saker is stealing from her own husband?"

"Exactly. Damien Saker didn't believe Sasha when she said it's actually Edwina who's been taking money from the till, so it's up to us to prove it."

"If I could snap a picture of Edwina with her hand in the till, do you think that would do the job?"

"That would definitely do the job."

"Then what are we waiting for!"

Once again Dooley and I were doing what we do best: taking a prolonged nap in Odelia's office, when suddenly her phone rang.

"Yes, Gran?" she said, picking up.

"I got the job!" Gran's voice could be heard screaming through the phone.

"That's great!"

"And guess what—Scarlett was hired, too!"

"Scarlett? What do you mean?"

"It's not much fun having no one to talk to, so I suggested that Scarlett join me on my job interview. And Damien must have taken a shine to Scarlett, cause it was actually him who hired us both!"

Uh-oh.

"We're starting tomorrow, bright and early. So wish us luck, honey!" And without awaiting Odelia's response, she disconnected.

Odelia slowly looked over to me, and I shrugged. "Unforeseen circumstances," I said.

"I just hope she won't screw it up," was Odelia's response.

"Do you think they'll get free cake to take home with them?" asked Dooley. "And free pie and cookies?"

But judging from Odelia's expression of concern, free pastry was the last thing on her mind. She then fixed me with a hopeful look. "Max, I think you better keep an eye on Gran and Scarlett. Make sure they don't do anything stupid."

And that's when I knew that my lazy days were over.

Chapter Three

And so the next morning, bright and early, as already indicated, Dooley and I were ready for our latest assignment: make sure that Gran and Scarlett exonerated Sasha Kay, and discovered who the real thief was, and didn't get into any trouble themselves.

It was an important job, and also a very responsible one. And so I decided not to let Odelia down, but to handle the assignment with the required diligence.

I'd actually been afraid that we wouldn't be allowed anywhere near the shop, since bakeries are in the business of dispensing food items, and take hygiene very seriously. And for some reason that I've never been able to fathom, they don't like pets in the shop.

But I shouldn't have worried, since Gran had told Damien that we were her support animals, and that she couldn't do a good job without us.

"What's a support animal, Max?" asked Dooley once we'd been officially installed in a corner of the bakery where we had a great overview of the entire operation.

"An animal that provides emotional support, Dooley."

"Oh, so we provide emotional support to Gran?"

"I guess we do. Or maybe it's just an excuse to get us into the bakery."

"I don't mind supporting Gran," he said. "Though if she falls down I'm not sure I'll be able to get her back on her feet."

It was actually funny to see Gran behind the counter at the bakery, and Scarlett, too. Both ladies were wearing colorful aprons, and after Edwina had showed them the ins and outs of operating the cash register, and how to box up the pies and cakes and handed them a list of prices of all the items for sale, they were good to go.

A voluminous woman walked into the store, and I recognized her as Gran's foe Ida Baumgartner, the hypochondriac.

"Oh, you're here now, are you?" said Ida, giving Gran and Scarlett one of those supercilious looks she does so well.

"Yes, I'm here," said Gran, giving Ida her most radiant smile. "So what was it you wanted?"

"Um, give me that banana pie over there, two chocolate éclairs, that lemon meringue pie, and throw in two almond croissants."

But Gran stood shaking her head. "Ida, Ida, Ida," she said reprovingly.

"What?" said Ida, surprised not to receive the kind of cooperation she expected.

"With your blood sugar level, and your cholesterol, I'm frankly surprised you'd even walk in here. What you need is a strictly sugar-free, fat-free diet. Hasn't Tex told you a million times?"

"But…"

"No more pie for you, Ida!"

"Well I never!"

"I'm just looking out for you."

"Vesta Muffin!" Ida cried. "You are potty!"

"And you are fat. Now go!"

Just then, Edwina walked in. "What's going on?" she asked, after directing a look at her best customer beating a disappointed retreat. "Didn't she want anything?"

"Oh, she wanted plenty," said Gran, "but I told her that with her diabetes and her high cholesterol it really was a bad idea to satisfy her pastry addiction."

Edwina's jaw dropped. "You did what?!"

"I saved a life today, Edwina," said Gran seriously, "and frankly I deserve a medal."

Edwina clearly wasn't in full agreement, because for the next five minutes she proceeded to berate Gran in very emphatic tones.

"Looks like Gran won't be saving any more lives," said Dooley.

"No, I guess not," I agreed.

The rest of the day passed more or less uneventfully. Ida, having received a phone call from Edwina, returned to pick up her chosen wares, giving Gran a look that spoke volumes, and if any of the other customers suffered from either diabetes, hypertension or whatever, Gran refrained from mentioning it or even doling out free medical advice.

A bakery is, after all, not a doctor's office. If people want to load up on sugar and fat, that's entirely their business.

The cast of characters at the bakery was as follows: apart

from Damien Saker and his wife Edwina, there was the son Ben who worked with his dad in the bakery, located at the back of the store, where the magic happened, and also baker's assistant Jeremy Fibber.

And since sleeping in the corner of a bakery shop isn't as peaceful as sleeping in the corner of a reporter's office, after almost having been stepped on by the umpteenth customer I decided to escape through the connecting door and go exploring a little.

Above the store, an apartment had been arranged, where the Saker family lived, and then of course there was the bakery itself, where large machines and equipment and ovens had been installed to create all that delicious stuff that was being sold in the shop.

My attention was attracted by loud voices that seemed to come from the apartment upstairs, and since I'm never too shy to stick my nose where it doesn't belong, and neither is Dooley, we walked up the stairs to take a closer look.

"Six hundred bucks for a dress!" Damien was saying at the top of his voice.

"A bargain," retorted his wife. "Or do you want me to look like a bag lady at the County Ball?"

"Your closet is full of dresses! You've got more dresses than a queen!"

"You really don't expect me to wear the same thing twice, do you? Besides, we can afford it."

"You're bleeding me dry, woman! And look at those shoes —they're not even nice!"

"That's because you have no sense of style. These are Jimmy Choos, Damien."

"Jimmy who?"

"They're the tip of the top in high fashion."

"Oh, my God," we heard Damien say, and then he came stomping out of what could only be the bedroom. Moments later his wife followed, and they both retreated into the kitchen, where they resumed their argument.

"They don't seem to get along very well, do they, Max?" said Dooley.

"No, they don't," I said.

"Good thing Odelia doesn't spend a fortune on dresses and shoes, or Chase would be unhappy, too."

"Odelia is much too sensible to spend all of her money on fancy clothes. Besides, I think she and Chase are saving."

"Saving? For what?"

I shrugged. "Beats me." They'd been putting money into a savings account, and I could regularly hear them talk about how much money had already accrued in the account.

"I'll bet it's to buy more kibble for us," said Dooley. "Or maybe they want to go on a cruise again."

I groaned. "I hope not." I didn't have a lot of happy memories about that cruise. Cats simply aren't made to float in a big metal box in the middle of the ocean. Then again, humans probably aren't either, but I guess their capacity for denial is greater than ours.

Damien Saker now came stomping out of the kitchen, and made his way down, and Dooley and I decided to take a closer look at this six-hundred-dollar dress.

The dress was lying on the bed, and it didn't look all that special to me. It was flimsy, and low-cut in both the front and the back, and if worn probably would show a lot of skin.

"There's not a lot of material, is there, Max?" said Dooley. "I think Edwina should ask her money back. She didn't get what she paid for."

"It isn't the amount of fabric that goes into a dress that determines the price, Dooley," I said. "It's the design."

"Oh," he said, giving the dress a puzzled look. Like me, Dooley isn't a big fan of high fashion, I guess. "But she'll be practically naked if she wears this dress, Max."

"That's probably the effect she's going for."

"I don't get it. If her husband doesn't like it, why wear it?"

"Somehow," I said, "I have the impression that it isn't her husband she wants to impress with this dress."

"Then who?"

"Your guess is as good as mine."

But at that moment Edwina came walking in, and when she saw us sitting on the bed next to her much-loved dress, she shooed us out.

ABOUT NIC

Nic has a background in political science and before being struck by the writing bug worked odd jobs around the world (including but not limited to massage therapist in Mexico, gardener in Italy, restaurant manager in India, and Berlitz teacher in Belgium).

When he's not writing he enjoys curling up with a good (comic) book, watching British crime dramas, French comedies or Nancy Meyers movies, sampling pastry (apple cake!), pasta and chocolate (preferably the dark variety), twisting himself into a pretzel doing morning yoga, going for a run, and spoiling his big red tomcat Tommy.

He lives with his wife (and aforementioned cat) in a small village smack dab in the middle of absolutely nowhere and is probably writing his next 'Mysteries of Max' book right now.

www.nicsaint.com

ALSO BY NIC SAINT

The Mysteries of Max
Purrfect Murder
Purrfectly Deadly
Purrfect Revenge
Purrfect Heat
Purrfect Crime
Purrfect Rivalry
Purrfect Peril
Purrfect Secret
Purrfect Alibi
Purrfect Obsession
Purrfect Betrayal
Purrfectly Clueless
Purrfectly Royal
Purrfect Cut
Purrfect Trap
Purrfectly Hidden
Purrfect Kill
Purrfect Boy Toy
Purrfectly Dogged
Purrfectly Dead
Purrfect Saint
Purrfect Advice
Purrfect Passion

A Purrfect Gnomeful
Purrfect Cover
Purrfect Patsy
Purrfect Son
Purrfect Fool
Purrfect Fitness
Purrfect Setup
Purrfect Sidekick
Purrfect Deceit
Purrfect Ruse
Purrfect Swing
Purrfect Cruise
Purrfect Harmony
Purrfect Sparkle
Purrfect Cure
Purrfect Cheat
Purrfect Catch
Purrfect Design
Purrfect Life
Purrfect Thief

The Mysteries of Max Omnibuses

Omnibus 1 (Books 1-3)
Omnibus 2 (Books 4-6)
Omnibus 3 (Books 7-9)
Omnibus 4 (Books 10-12)
Omnibus 5 (Books 13-15)
Omnibus 6 (Books 16-18)
Omnibus 7 (Books 19-21)

Omnibus 8 (Books 22-24)

Omnibus 9 (Books 25-27)

Omnibus 10 (Books 28-30)

Omnibus 11 (Books 31-33)

Omnibus 12 (Books 34-36)

Omnibus 13 (Books 37-39)

The Mysteries of Max Shorts

Purrfect Santa (3 shorts in one)

Purrfectly Flealess

Purrfect Wedding

Nora Steel

Murder Retreat

The Kellys

Murder Motel

Death in Suburbia

Emily Stone

Murder at the Art Class

Washington & Jefferson

First Shot

Alice Whitehouse

Spooky Times

Spooky Trills

Spooky End

Spooky Spells

Ghosts of London
Between a Ghost and a Spooky Place
Public Ghost Number One
Ghost Save the Queen
Box Set 1 (Books 1-3)
A Tale of Two Harrys
Ghost of Girlband Past
Ghostlier Things

Charleneland
Deadly Ride
Final Ride

Neighborhood Witch Committee
Witchy Start
Witchy Worries
Witchy Wishes

Saffron Diffley
Crime and Retribution
Vice and Verdict
Felonies and Penalties (Saffron Diffley Short 1)

The B-Team
Once Upon a Spy

Tate-à-Tate
Enemy of the Tates

Ghosts vs. Spies
The Ghost Who Came in from the Cold

Witchy Fingers

Witchy Trouble

Witchy Hexations

Witchy Possessions

Witchy Riches

Box Set 1 (Books 1-4)

The Mysteries of Bell & Whitehouse

One Spoonful of Trouble

Two Scoops of Murder

Three Shots of Disaster

Box Set 1 (Books 1-3)

A Twist of Wraith

A Touch of Ghost

A Clash of Spooks

Box Set 2 (Books 4-6)

The Stuffing of Nightmares

A Breath of Dead Air

An Act of Hodd

Box Set 3 (Books 7-9)

A Game of Dons

Standalone Novels

When in Bruges

The Whiskered Spy

ThrillFix

Homejacking

The Eighth Billionaire

The Wrong Woman

Printed in Great Britain
by Amazon